(continued from front flap)

Other contributions include fiction by Carol Jane Bangs, Ursule Molinaro, Bradford Morrow, Henry H. Roth, and Harriet Zinnes, and poetry by Edwin Brock (England), Rüdiger Kremer (West Germany), Ernest Kroll, John Frederick Nims, Jean Orizet (France), Peter Reading (England), Anthony Robbins, Kirk Robertson, and Richard Sieburth.

"*Sui generis* now among commercial trade publishers, New Directions' annual roundup is just what this sort of non-textbook anthology ought to be...." —*Kirkus Reviews*

"...the New Directions anthologies have always been at the forefront of avant-garde writing." —*Booklist*

[Also available: *New Directions 17,* New Directions Paperbook 103; *ND18,* Cloth; *ND19,* Cloth; *ND21, Cloth; ND22,* Cloth; *ND23,* Cloth; *ND24,* NDP332; *ND25,* Cloth; *ND26,* Cloth; *ND27,* Cloth & NDP359; *ND28,* Cloth; *ND29,* Cloth; *ND30,* Cloth; *ND31,* Cloth; *ND32,* Cloth; *ND33,* Cloth; *ND34,* Cloth; *ND35,* Cloth; *ND36,* Cloth & NDP449; *ND37,* Cloth; *ND38,* Cloth; *ND39,* Cloth; *ND40,* Cloth & NDP500; *ND41,* Cloth & NDP505; *ND42,* Cloth & NDP510; *ND43,* Cloth & NDP524; *ND44,* Cloth & NDP537; *ND45,* Cloth & NDP541; *ND46,* Cloth & NDP553; *ND47,* Cloth & NDP560; *ND48,* Cloth & NDP579; *ND49,* Cloth & NDP609; *ND50,* NDP623; *ND51,* Cloth & NDP644.]

NEW DIRECTIONS 52

In memoriam

ROBERT DUNCAN
1919–1988

New Directions in Prose and Poetry 52

Edited by J. Laughlin

with Peter Glassgold and Griselda Ohannessian

 A New Directions Book

ACKNOWLEDGMENTS
Grateful acknowledgment is made to the editors and publishers of magazines and newspapers in which some of the material in this volume first appeared: for Edwin Brock, *Ambit* (London); for Michael McClure, *Poetry Flash;* for Bradford Morrow, *Bomb* (Copyright © 1987 by New Art Publications, Inc.); for John Frederick Nims, *The New Criterion* (Copyright © 1986 by John Frederick Nims); for Jerome Rothenberg, *Sulfur* (Copyright © 1988 by Sulfur); for George Steiner, *The Times Literary Supplement* (Copyright © 1988 by George Steiner).

Carmel Bird's "Every Home Should Have a Cedar Chest" was first published in *Soft Lounger* (1985), an anthology edited by Antonia Bruns and John Jenkins and brought out by Fringe Newtwork (Australia). Section I from "Ash Wednesday" in *Collected Poems 1909–1962* by T. S. Eliot (Copyright 1936 by Harcourt Brace Jovanovich, Inc.; Copyright © 1963, 1964 by T. S. Eliot) is reprinted by permission of the publisher. Joel Oppenheimer's "The Uses of Adversity" was originally published as a booklet by The Zelot Press, Vandergrift, Pennsylvania (1987). Jean Orizet's "Four Poems," first published in *Tiers of Survival: Selected Poems* by Jean Orizet, translated by Aletha Reed DeWees (English Translation Copyright © 1984 by Mundus Artium Press), are reprinted by permission of Mundus Artium Press, Richardson, Texas. Peter Reading's "Five Poems," first published in *Ukelele Music* and *Stet* (Copyright © 1985, 1986 by Peter Reading), are reprinted by permission of Secker and Warburg (London). "Initiations" by Kirk Robertson, previously collected in *Origins, Initiations* (Copyright © 1980 by Kirk Robertson), Turkey Press, Isla Vista, California, is reprinted by permission of the author. Richard Sieburth's "Weights and Measures" was first published by Ulysse Fin de Siècle, Paris (1987).

Manufactured in the United States of America
New Directions Books are published on acid-free paper.
First published clothbound (ISBN: 0–8112–1076–6) and as New Directions Paperbook 664 (ISBN: 0–8112–1077–4) in 1988
Published simultaneously in Canada by Penguin Books Canada Limited

New Directions Books are published for James Laughlin
by New Directions Publishing Corporation,
80 Eighth Avenue, New York 10011

CONTENTS

ROBERT DUNCAN:
A MODERN ROMANTIC

MICHAEL McCLURE

RE
-turn.   In spring-up green freshet
turn.   Delight to the eye . . .

Robert Duncan was everything we believed him to be. The savant and soul-maker of recent years who so many of us saw in poetry readings and his lectures at the New College was the flowering of an earlier Duncan. But Duncan's flowering was continual, and as long ago as 1954 Duncan had an enormous body of energy and genius that he exerted. As the students of his first workshop at San Francisco State listened to his insights and projections regarding their poems and looked in wonder at his restructuring of their work on the blackboard, they knew something big was happening. Duncan was one of the pantheon that was pre-Beat and pre-San Francisco Renaissance and one of the heroes who walked the earth with Rexroth, Everson, Madeleine Gleason, James Broughton, Jack Spicer, and Robin Blaser. Those were not the good old days, but the sinister cold Fifties. Duncan had been part of the World War II anarchist circles; he'd edited outspoken magazines and published a booklength poem; he'd dressed in peasant blouses and workman's boots—he'd rubbed shoulders with Anais Nin and Henry Miller and Kenneth Patchen. He had announced his homosexuality—in defiance of the wall of silence. He'd become domestic, one of a couple, and

1

what he called a householder, with Jess (who studied with Clyfford Still and had turned to Romantic landscape painting).

Duncan was a man with nerve. In an era that twitched with dismay at the thought of having influences, he called himself a derivative poet, and he found a clear, early voice in a book of Gertrude Stein imitations. His sources ranged from Dante and Zukofsky to children's books. He was writing poetry that was so breathtaking in its intellectual excitement and vivacity and so technically thrilling in its shape and structure that one hardly knew how to discuss the poems. In his book *Letters,* "Light Song" begins:

> ;husbands   the hand   the keys   a free imp-
>   rovisation keeping the constant vow . . .

We were left in a state of pleasurable awe that this most trembling, in-looking world-lover—with one eye near-sighted and the other far-sighted—was opening a door for those who chose to pass through it. Robert reiterated to all who listened that there were new voices and a new sound in poetry, and he put Levertov, Creeley, and Olson out there for anyone to see and to hear. In those days, Duncan gave solo readings of his music drama, *Faust Foutu*—for which he'd composed the music and for which he invented the voices of all the characters. Today, those jovial readings would be called performance art.

This wildly capricious man had the unflinching politics of a William Blake-like visionary and was opposed to any form of fascism or totalitarianism or philistinism, or command of involuntary restriction or constriction of the living child in man or woman. In Duncan's apparent scatteredness was a solid, growing core of old-fashioned character and personal soundness that is not often seen. People around Robert wondered where the wisdom came from, where the fountain of unrelenting demands for liberty had its source, and what were the subtle sources of his swift and accurate opinions and decisions.

Thirty-five years ago this very, very modern Romantic poet had his pen at the pulses of what was meaningful—and he was beginning to allow the flood of his art to flow into varied channels and streams and shapes—as in his ongoing "Passages" and "Structure of Rime" as well as the individual books. Duncan saw the flowing universe of language, and he let that be the shape of his songs, poems, odes, as they bubbled out separately from their secret springs and then joined in rivers and pools and channeled to water-falls and wordfalls.

In the Bay Area in the Fifties, and for a while after that, a young poet could sense that his older artist mentors had been reading Kropotkin's anarchist philosophy in *Mutual Aid*. Kenneth Rexroth might help a young poet move all his family belongings to a new flat; in fact, Rexroth might be the one to lug a huge stove up three flights of stairs. Artist Ronald Bladen might contribute his scant earnings to finance a literary magazine. Almost everyone who could worked at some job or craft or was a merchant seaman—and probably no one expected and financial remuneration from their art. Duncan did typing of thesis manuscripts and hitchhiked across the Bay to U.C. to pick up the manuscripts. One could often see him there at the bridge ramp, radiating his energy, with thumb out to the air. In the evening, he and Jess would be hosts to hopeful writers and filmmakers and painters. Robert gave generously of his mind and his imagination, and unlike many poets he liberated those who wanted to listen so they could be themselves, and not writers in Robert's manner.

Robert had much pride, but it was not hurt pride or false pride; it was pride in his art and life, and the arts and lives of his friends. At one point, my family and I were so sick with flu and poverty that Robert and Jess swooped down on us, took us away, and nursed us back to health. And I often saw Robert's intuitive understanding of infants and children in his friendship with my daughter. Duncan was surrounded by a younger generation of men and women who wanted to understand the glamour and mystery of life as he saw it and lived it. Though that generation must have seemed dense-headed sometimes, Robert kept laughing, telling stories, and reading new poems, while we sat as if enchanted, and the bookshelves in Robert's parlor sagged, heavy with more and more that he was studying, from the *Zohar* and Sapir to George MacDonald.

When I think of Robert, I see firelight in a hearth and bronze Art Deco women with long hair, and Oz books and cats and San Francisco fog and Jackson Pollock. I think of him recounting some recent discovery in the sciences, and as he tells the technical details of a rat overpopulation experiment it becomes the story of London and

Peking—and then it exfoliates to be, in a visionary way, a vast set of perceptions of the physical universe. Then, for a moment, I see Robert explicating Pound's *Cantos* line by line. Then Robert is exploring Whitehead's or Plato's philosophy. Then Robert is boundlessly denouncing a poet he believes is untrue to poetry. Then Robert is telling a story about H.D. or Laura Riding.

Then I can smell the saffron that Robert adds to the first bouillabaise I ever saw anyone make—tentacles of squid and pieces of a white fish and chunks of red fish and clams. Artists were poor in those days, and a rich soup wasn't something one got at a stylish restaurant but something one scrimped for to celebrate with. Robert was even poorer than some others, in dollars, because he was always buying paintings and books by other artists and writers. It was a rich world made with little money, before the Vietnam War brought our wealth of plastic cars and plastic televisions, and suet-and-petroleum gendered fast foods.

Robert had grown up in California; he was moved by the California landscape of chaparral and oak savannah and meadow flowers. Seeing a beautiful orange California poppy, he'd pick the ripe seedcase and put it in his pocket to plant the seed in his garden. He was always working the ground and opening the fields and meadows and glades inside of himself, as the titles of his books tell. Surely an old man can be a flowering of the young man, and somehow, in some Jungian sense, if he individuates himself, then he can be like the big, simple, glorious flowers of the tulip trees that were blossoming in San Francisco on the day Robert died.

San Francisco has always been a literary province in the eyes of Easterners living in the overpopulation centers. As artists, we did not want to be provincial; we wanted to be modernists, and more than that we did not want to be San Francisco artists, or Bay Area artists, or California artists, or West Coast artists, or American artists; we wanted to be *artists* without all those qualifiers. As brilliant and as "major" as Rexroth was, it was Duncan who seemed to be even more international. It did not matter that Duncan was unknown or that he said he'd be happy to have just five hundred readers—the scope of intention and smoldering liveliness in his poems made Duncan seem to be the most international among us. We could imagine Robert speaking with Picasso and Cocteau and Stein and D. H. Lawrence.

But also Duncan was a time-diver. He could dive back through time into the medieval history he studied, or he could learn French and commune with Baudelaire. Or Robert would take the course of extolling Shelley, as if he were with us, and rewrite Shelley's long lyric *Arethusa*.

In the days I'm describing in Robert's life, I was listening to Brahms recordings, and the album jackets portrayed an old man with longish hair and a white beard. One day I found a photo of Brahms as a handsome, cleanshaven, almost winsome young man, and I took a bust of Brahms and attached the picture of the young Brahms to the old bearded face of the bust, and I gave it to a friend. Like the photo of the younger Brahms, Duncan was a good-looking man in the years of his early maturity; sometimes he was stocky, sometimes slender, sometimes plump. Robert would have a period of casual dressing and then move into a time of neckties and vests and charcoal suits. In his middle age he became a serious dresser—he'd sit in his front room with a stack of books about him and his pen and notebook at hand, with Scriabin or Stravinsky on the record player.

Robert could always fall into a powerful, driven, self-centered way of speaking, and as he grew into the Seventies and Eighties the scope of his wordplay broadened like the deep language world he was forever exploring in his unspoken consciousness. Robert trembled as he moved onto a subject, and then the subject changed to another and then another, and as he knit them all together in his mind he shook—his hands shook—and his eyes looked in different directions. Year by year Duncan came to seem more patrician, like some groomed lord of poetry and thinking. He seemed superhuman, and at the same time the most human.

An old friend of Robert's believes that this is the end of an era; she said that Robert formed her ideas of painting. An admirer of Robert's who is a designer and printer says that Robert gave him the image of what art is because he perceived Robert moving into poetry and becoming the art. On going to visit Duncan there was the feeling that one was meeting with someone like Yeats or Joyce or Nerval or Villon—one felt that just before entering, Duncan might have been communing with the troubador Peire Vidal or Emily Dickinson. There was a luminosity about Robert, and it grew with each decade as he lived in the aura—not really seeking it—and he always lit it up with his unexpected smile and his spontaneous merry laugh.

KHURBN

An excerpt

JEROME ROTHENBERG

DOS OYSLEYDIKN (THE EMPTYING)

> *Since the hidden is bottomless, totality is more invisible than visible. (C.E.)*

1
at honey street in ostrowa
where did the honey people go?
empty   empty
miodowa empty
empty bakery & empty road to warsaw
yellow wooden houses & houses plastered up with stucco
the shadow of an empty name still on their doors
shadai & shadow shattering the mother tongue
the mother's tongue but empty
the way the streets are empty where we walk
pushing past crowds of children
old women airing themselves outside the city hall
old farmers riding empty carts down empty roads
who don't dispel but make an emptiness
a taste of empty honey
empty rolls you push your fingers through

empty sorrel soup dribbling from their empty mouths
defining some other poland
lost to us the way the moon
is lost to us
the empty clock tower measuring her light four ways
sorrel in gardens mother of god at roadsides
in the reflection of the empty trains
only the cattle bellow in
like jews the dew-eyed wanderers
still present   still the flies
cover their eyeballs
the trains drive eastward, falling
down a hole (a holocaust) of empty houses
of empty ladders leaning against haystacks no one climbs
empty ostrowa & empty ostroleka
old houses empty in the woods near wyzkow
dachas the peasants would rent to you
& sleep in stables
the bialo forest spreading to every side
retreating the closer we come to it to claim it
empty oaks & empty fir trees
a man in an empty ditch who reads a book
the way the jews once read
in the cold polish light   the fathers sat there too
the mothers posed at the woods' edge
the road led brightly to treblinka
& other towns   beaches at brok
along the bug
marshes with cat tails
cows tied to trees
past which their ghosts walk
their ghosts refuse to walk
tomorrow in empty fields of poland
still cold against their feet
an empty pump black water drips from
will form a hill of ice
the porters will dissolve wth burning sticks
they will find a babe's face at the bottom
invisible & frozen imprinted in the rock

2
"PRACTICE YOUR SCREAM"   I SAID
(why did I say it?)
because it was his scream & wasn't my own
it hovered between us   bright
to our senses always bright it held
the center place
then somebody else came up & stared
deep in his eyes there found a memory
of horses galloping faster the wheels dyed red
behind them   the poles had reserved
a feast day but the jew
locked in his closet screamed
into his vest a scream
that had no sound   therefore
spiraled around the world
so wild that it shattered stones
it made the shoes piled in the doorway
scatter their nails   things testify
—the law declares it—
shoes & those dearer objects
like hair & teeth do
by their presence
I cannot say that they share the pain
or show it not even the photos
in which the expressions of the dead shine forth
the crutches by their mass the prosthetic limbs by theirs
bear witness the eyeglasses bear witness
the suitcases the children's shoes the german tourists
in the stage set oswieczim had become
the letters over its gates still glowing
still writ large
arbeit macht frei
& to the side   HOTEL
and GASTRONOMIC BAR
the spirit of the place dissolving
indifferent to his presence
there with the other ghosts
the uncle   grieving

his eyelids turning brown an eye
protruding from his rump
this man whose body
is a crab's
his gut turned outward
the pink flesh of his children
hanging from him
that his knees slide up against
there is no holocaust
for these   but khurban only
the word still spoken by the dead
who say   my khurban
& my children's khurban
it is the only word that the poem allows
because it is their own
the word as prelude to the scream
it enters
through the asshole
circles along the gut
into the throat
& breaks out
in a cry   a scream
no one can hear but me
it is his scream that shakes me
weeping   in oswieczim
& that allows the poem to come

3
spirits of the dead   lights
flickering (he said) their ruakh
will never leave the earth
instead they crowd the forests the fields
around the privies the hapless spirits
wait millions of souls
turned into ghosts at once
the air is full of them
they are standing each one beside a tree
under its shadows or the moon's
but they cast no shadows of their own

this moment & the next they are pretending
to be rocks   but who is fooled
who is fooled here   by the dead   the jews
the gypsies   the leadeyed polish patriot
living beings reduced to symbols
of what it had been to be alive
"o do not touch them" the mother cries
fitful, as almost in a dream
she draws the child's hand to her heart
in terror   but the innocent dead
grow furious they break down doors
drop slime onto your tables
they tear their tongues out by the roots
& smear your lamps your children's lips
with blood a hole drilled in the wall
will not deter them
from stolen homes stone architectures
they hate they are the convoys of the dead
the ghostly drivers still searching
the roads to malkin   ghost carts overturned
ghost autos in blue ditches
if only our eyes were wild enough
to see them our hearts to know their terror
terror of saturdays & terror of wednesdays
the terror of the man who walks alone
their victim whose house whose skin
they crawl in   incubus & succubus
a dibbuk leaping from a cow to lodge inside
his throat   clusters of jews
who swarm here fathers without hair
blackbearded mothers
they lap up fire   water   slime
entangle the hairs of brides
or mourn their clothing hovering
over a field of rags   half-rotted shoes
& tablecloths   old thermos bottles   rings
lost tribes in empty synagogues
at night their voices
carrying across the fields (caw caw)

to rot your kasha your barley
stricken beneath their acid rains
your bison screaming
delivering their curses against the land
no holocaust because no sacrifice
no sacrifice to give the lie
of meaning   & no meaning   after auschwitz
there is only poetry   no hope
no other language left to heal
no language   & no faces
because no faces left   no names
no sudden recognitions on the street
only the dead still swarming   only khurban
a dead man in a rabbi's clothes
who squats   outside the mortuary house
who guards their privies who is called
master of shit   an old alarm clock
hung around his neck   who holds
a wreath of leaves under his nose
from eden   "to drive out
"the stinking odor of this world"

NOTE: In 1987 I was a decade, more, past *Poland/1931*. I went
to Poland for the first time & to the small town, Ostrow-Mazowiecz,
sixty miles northeast of Warsaw, from which my parents had come
in 1920. The town was there & the street, Miodowa (meaning
"honey"), where my father's parents had a bakery. I hadn't realized
that the town was only fifteen miles from Treblinka, and when we
went there (as we had to), there was only an empty field & the
thousands of large stones that make up the memorial. We were the
only ones there except for a group of three people—another family
perhaps—who seemed to be picnicking at the side. This was in sharp
contrast to the crowds of mostly German tourists at Auschwitz (Os-
wieczim) & to the fullness of that other Poland that I had once
imagined. The absence of the living seemed to create a vacuum in
which the dead were free to speak. It wasn't the first time that I

thought of poetry as the language of the dead, but never as inescapably as now. Those in my own family had died without a trace—with one exception: an uncle who had gone to the woods with a group of Jewish partisans and who, when he heard that his wife and children were murdered at Treblinka, drank himself blind in a deserted cellar & blew his brains out. That, anyway, was how the story had come back to us, a long time before I ever heard a word like holocaust. It was a word with which I never felt at home: too Christian & too beautiful, too much smacking of a "sacrifice" I didn't & still don't understand. The word with which we spoke of it was the Yiddish-Hebrew word, khurban, & it was this word that was with me all the time we stayed in Poland. When I was writing *Poland/1931*, at a great distance from the place, I decided deliberately that it was not to be a poem about the "holocaust." There was a reason for that, I think, as there is now for allowing my uncle's khurban to speak through me. The poems that I first began to hear at Treblinka are the clearest message I have ever gotten about why I write poetry. They are an answer also to the proposition—by Adorno & others—that poetry cannot or should not be written after Auschwitz. Our search since then has been for the origins of poetry, not as a willful desire to wipe the slate clean, but as a recognition of those other voices & the scraps of poems they left behind them in the mud.

ONE-MINUTE STORIES

ISTVÁN ÖRKÉNY

Translated from the Hungarian by Judith Sollosy

PROFESSIONAL PRIDE

I'm not made of putty.

I know how to control myself.

Though long years of assiduous labor, the recognition of my talent—my entire future, in fact—lay in the balance, I kept a straight face.

"I'm an animal artist, I said.

"What can you do?" the impresario asked.

"I can imitate the song of birds."

"I'm sorry," he shrugged, "that's old hat."

"Old hat? The cooing of the dove? The piping of the reed sparrow? The calling of the quail? The screeching of the sea gull? The trill of the nightingale?"

"Passé," said the impresario, suppressing a yawn.

"Good bye, then," said I politely, and flew out the open window.

CLASSIFIED ADVERTISEMENT

Nostalgia
"Must urgently exchange (money no object) my two-and-a-half room, fifth-floor apartment with built-in kitchen cabinets overlooking Eagle Peak from Joliot Curie Square for a two-and-a-half room, fifth-floor apartment with built-in kitchen cabinets overlooking Eagle Peak from Joliot Curie Square."

NEWS
Last night, miner Márton Haris of Borsodbánya smoked in bed. After finishing his cigarette he switched off his lamp, turned to the wall, and fell fast asleep.

SEAL

THE DEATH OF THE ACTOR

This afternoon, on a side street off Ulloi út, the popular actor Zoltán Zetelaki collapsed and lost consciousness.

Passers-by rushed him to a nearby clinic, but despite the application of the latest advances in medical science, including the use of an iron lung, all efforts to revive him were in vain. At six-thirty in the evening, after lengthy agony, the outstanding actor passed away. His body was immediately transferred to the Institute of Anatomy.

Despite this sad occurrence, tonight's performance of *King Lear* was held as usual. Though Zetelaki was a few moments late and looked rather worn-out during the first act (here and there he clearly had to rely on the prompter), he gradually revived and was so convincing as the dying king that the audience applauded in the middle of his scene.

Afterward, Zetelaki was invited to dinner but declined. "Thank you," he said, "but I've had a rather trying day."

THE INTERPOLATION

Dénes Dénes, the representative universally acclaimed for his proposals and interpolations of public interest, was once again preparing a major bill for the day's meeting of Parliament. Yesterday he had busied himself collecting facts, and this morning, too, he could think of nothing else as he sipped his coffee in bed.

But—because he was so preoccupied, perhaps—the representative from Csenger County got the sequence of events confused. Instead of first taking his bath, he addressed his proposal to end the drought not to Parliament, but to his wife and two teenage sons, in the bathroom. His family was unanimously in favor of the proposal.

In Parliament, however, when it was his turn to speak, he went up to the speaker's platform, but instead of delivering his interpolation in the interest of bettering the future of his drought-ridden district, he took a hot bath. He got into the tub, lathered his ears, neck, underarms, and loins, and then, after showering and drying himself off, sat back down in the seat tradition had assigned him as Csenger County's representative.

After a short debate which included a speech by the Minister of Agriculture, Representative Dénes's bill was unanimously approved and enacted into law. (*Hungarian Telegraph Office*)

THE CHAUFFEUR

József Pereszlényi, acquisitions man, brought his Wartburg (Lic. No. CO 75-14) to halt in front of the corner newspaper stand.

"Give me today's *Budapest Herald*."

"I'm all out."

"Fine. Give me yesterday's, then."

"I'm all out of yesterday's, too. But I happen to have tomorow's."

"Has it got the movie program?"

"They all have it."

"Good. Give me tomorrow's paper, then," said the acquisitions man.

He got back in his car. He found the movie program. After a while, he spotted a Czechoslovak film, *The Loves of a Blonde*, which he'd heard praised. It was playing at the Blue Lagoon on Golgotha Street, and the next show was at five-thirty.

That gave him plenty of time. He continued thumbing through tomorrow's paper. He came across a small item about acquisitions man József Pereszlényi, whose Wartburg (Lic. No. CO 75-14) exceeded the speed limit, and not far from the Blue Lagoon movie theater on Golgotha Street, collided head-on with a truck. The incautious acquisitions man died on the spot.

"Well, I'll be darned," said Pereszlényi to no one in particular.

He glanced at his watch. It was almost five-thirty. He shoved the newspaper in his pocket and, exceeding the speed limit, ran his car head-on into a truck on Golgotha Street, not far from the Blue Lagoon movie theater.

He died on the spot with tomorrow's paper in his pocket.

EROTICISM

It was a great day for Zsolozmai. He had written a review of a popular play that everybody had praised. But he pointed out that the work is full of licentious innuendos, in actual fact its dialogues are erotic discharges, and in this pansexual atmosphere, even the two wings of the curtain seem to fornicate as they fall.

Zsolozsmai himself led a life of chastity. He had barely seen his own naked body. He took his baths in a long white nightshirt in which there was a slit in the crucial spot, just as there was one in his wife's nightgown. In this way they were able to bring their three children into the world without any filth to speak of.

This review rocketed Zsolozsmai to the top of his career. He strolled—nay, floated!—down Rákóczi út in the highest of spirits. He didn't even mind the pornographic signs that populated the street: policemen with outstretched arms, advertising pillars (yuck!), and anyone who's ever seen dogs go at it knows what these articulated buses are up to as they come to a sudden stop. Indeed, he would've taken all this in stride, but further off, in front of a shop window, he came to a halt.

A young girl stood behind the glass pane, clad only in a two-piece bikini, holding a big red ball above her head. The girl was made of wax, but Zsolozsmai was all ashiver. He concluded that the girl's nudity was disgusting. He concluded that (for some mysterious reason) her lasciviousness was only heightened by the ball she held above her head. He further concluded that (strange as it may seem) the girl had winked at him.

Instead of walking away, Zsolozsmai shyly tipped his hat. Then, in his embarrassment forgetting that he had already done so, he tipped it once again. This made the girl laugh invitingly. She shook the price tag from her limbs, crashed through the window, and flung herself at Zsolozsmai.

Though the critic broke into a run, he could not shake his pursuer. Several passers-by followed suit, and by the time they reached the Hotel Astoria, a fight broke out. Thinking that he was witnessing a political about-face, the newsboy on the corner began to shout the names of prewar newspapers like *New Nation* and *Dawn's Early Light*. This just added fuel to the fire, but unheeding, the girl in the bikini continued pursuit of her prey all the way to the university, through the gate, up the stairs, and into a lecture room. There she wrestled Zsolozsmai down to the floor and addressed him thus:

"OOOOH, I JUST ADORE YOUR CUTE LITTLE NOSE, PROFESSOR!"

And with that, she kissed Zsolozsmai—a Kossuth Prize recipient!—on the tip of his nose and went back to the store window.

THE RIGHT TO REMAIN STANDING

If now the conductress who (as if by chance) has already looked me up and down several times should happen to say, will all passengers kindly move to the back of the bus, then I, you can bet your life, wouldn't so much as open my mouth, nor would I move, I'd remain standing right where I am, as if my feet were rooted to the ground. I have a very good reason for standing here, namely, I've got my briefcase down here, resting against my ankle, with a six-pack of beer, ten pairs of franks, mustard, bread, butter, cheese, and a bottle of three-star brandy weighing thirteen to seventeen pounds in all, and I'm not about to move it. On the contrary, I'm lucky if the briefcase doesn't tip over each time the driver slams his foot on the brake. Of course, all this is happening because there are always unpredictable, insufferable, hysterical people in the world like my best friends, who insist on waiting till the last minute to invite themselves to dinner. On the other hand, I can't very well explain that here, I'd make a fool of myself in front of the other passengers. So I will just mutely but stubbornly stay right where I am.

Now then, should the conductress (and this is not entirely out of the question) happen to address me, saying, will that gentleman in the gray raincoat kindly make room for the boarding passengers, I'd be forced, politely but explicitly, to say, dear madame, you'd do better to shut up.

If upon hearing this the conductress (and this could easily be the case) should then chance to answer, how dare you talk to me like that, then I'd say, still politely, or if not politely, with a certain cool reserve, dear madame, turn blue in the face, choke on your own spittle, and above all, shut your trap, because all you do is lecture, annoy, and insult the passengers, and if after this (such things have been known to happen) she should retort, if you dare say one more word in that tone of voice, sir, I shall be forced to call a cop, I'd counter with, dear madame, you can call the army, the navy, an entire armored division, for all I care, I will not budge one iota from this place, to which I have as much right as anybody else.

Now then, provided she could call a cop at all and the cop could fight his way onto this crowded bus and confront me, then I'd say, calm, collected but determined, I'd say, look here, friend, why don't you go to the devil, to which he (and this is also within the realm of possibility) should happen to answer, if you insist on using this tone of voice, sir, I shall be obliged to take you in, then I—after all, even my patience has its limits—would say, dear friend, you're not taking me anywhere if you know what's good for you, otherwise I might end up using your belly for a trampoline, bouncing on it up and down until all the breath's gone, and you won't feel like threatening me anymore.

And if after this (which is only to be expected) the police captain questioning me should happen to lecture me saying, look here, sir, you seem like a man of learning, your clothes and demeanor betray a man of sound sense, how could you say such a thing to a police officer who was only doing his duty when he took a poor working woman under his protection who was only doing her duty, too, and with the utmost courtesy, I might add, well, this I wouldn't even deign to answer, I'd back up a step, unzip my fly, and pee on the ink-stained, greasy, institution-gray carpet on the floor of the police station, and after having thus relieved myself and zipping up my pants, at most I'd say, see, captain, there's my answer, and if after this (and this is still within the realm of possibility) the chief physician of the psychiatric ward should, with mock indulgence, instruct me to close my eyes, stretch out my arms, and walk down an imaginary line in his direction, I wouldn't close my eyes, I wouldn't stretch forth my arms, but I'd start down that imaginary line toward him as sure as hell and kick him in the stomach so hard, he'd do a double flip over the top of his desk.

And that's just for starters. Because if after this the muscular male nurse who's been standing behind me should throw himself at me and try to restrain me, I, who wouldn't be taken unaware, would kick him in the shin so hard, he'd fall flat on his back, and I'd fling myself at him, pin him down, and gouge out his eyes by pressing my two thumbs, starting from the corners of his eyes into the sockets, making his eyeballs squirm right out with a soft pop. After this, just to make sure, I'd bash his brains in, and now, free to go, I'd grab my briefcase, go out to the street, hail a cab, and reaching home just in time, greet my guests with my customary hospitality.

HISTORICAL MISTAKE

"Hello! Moloko?"

"Excuse me?"

"Moloko?"

"Vy po-russki govorite?"

"I don't understand."

"I don't understand either, madame."

"I want to speak to my son-in-law."

"In that case, why did you ask for moloko?"

"Why shouldn't I?"

"Because it's Russian for milk."

"But that's what I call my son-in-law."

"That's not me."

"But I'm sure I called the right number."

"There must be some mistake, then, madame."

THREE POEMS

EDWIN BROCK

IN THE BEGINNING

She is a triangle
like Britannia

she keeps the walls
of her room waiting

you do not know
when she arrives

nor will you know
when she leaves

the walls are sycophants
and repeat her like dummies.

Through a window
memory is breaking the rod

which is not spared
to spoil a child

I cannot go inside
the walls will report me

I will lean through the glass
and shout back:

Blood is thinner than water
and flows more freely.

And under the sky
which is as neutral as money

under that sky
make this enemy

as the foundations tremble
and the walls crack.

THAT BEAUTY, THIS BEAST

It is that moment
in a story or a poem
when he goes
for the first time, alone,
to her room

and the fantasies
that have seen you through
your life begin.

There is the locked door,
white sheets upon
a single bed,
fireglow and footprints
in the snow all over Europe

as though crossing these frontiers
this touching overcomes
inheritance and language.

There are the words
you cannot hear
(there is always something
before the first thing
you remember) and the
beckoning which disturbs
like an interrupted dream.

You do not enter
(the spider is on the wall,
the eyeless teddy-bear
by your side): barefoot
upon the same cold stair
you strain to hear
the breathing of an Eden
you did not know
and cannot share.

A LESSON IN ECONOMICS

To make bread you take
flour, water, yeast, some
salt and bake it. To catch
fish you hang a line where
fish are and drag them out.
Historically it is better
if the loaves are made from
barley and the fish dried
but probably any fish and bread
will do and there are
excellent ones in Sainsbury's,
The difficulty begins when
even with 3 million unemployed
you cannot find 5000 hungry
people to watch you break
the bread and divide the fish

This miracle became redundant
2000 years ago, and was
never popular. A few people
still meet to talk and sing
about it and you can't blame
them for that nor for the way
they drive home afterwards.
Nobody's sorrier than they
are about the way the bread
the fish and the people will not
get up and walk around but
they know that even if they did
somebody would gather them up
and sell them back for
a week's work and that
somehow there will always be
about 3 million unemployed.

FOUR POEMS

JEAN ORIZET

Translated from the French by Aletha Reed DeWees

THE SWALLOW OF SIDI BOU SAID

It appeared at the moment when the muezzin's chanting voice made the call to evening prayer.

At first, perpendicular to the Café des Nattes, it seemed immobile, but a light breeze spliced it into the headway, and in a second's span its wingline joined the horizon's.

Descending again, it made a flickering note on whitened walls and blue moucharabieh.

The smell of jasmine rode the air; warm fog was groping up from Carthage when the swallow swooped toward the port and became again that sail whose shape the magic of the place had allowed it momentarily to put aside.

WINTER ON THE BALTIC

For Ursula and J. J. Kéourédon

Baltic, tranquil lake with glints of old bronze swallowed at a few cable lengths by fog. Following the shore a line of trees carved in pristine hoarfrost incises with a keener edge than the shore's the gray snow, scaly on flat fields. Colorless sand where ducks, gulls, and waterhens are the only bathers at this late date in January. Temperature: fifteen degrees below zero.

They say that in more rigorous winters, the sea freezes over. Swans are sometimes caught by surprise. If no one comes to free them, they die with necks extended, smooth jewels set in aquamarine.

PRESUMPTIVE SITE OF SODOM

Lower than the level of any sea it lingers: the Dead Sea dying in the fastness of a fault where Sodom one day disappeared.

What resembles from a distance the flotsam of sea spume is only crystallized salt.

The sea basks unmoving in sulfurous heat; teasingly shows its skeleton under the petrified eyes of Lot's wife, that sentinel of nothingness.

GOLD RUSH

Autumn ascendant. From the mill at Longchamp to the towers of La Défense, bronzed steel and inundated glass owe their colors to the death of leaves—death without reality since their exposed ribs lend wild vividness to the city.

They wrangle over mother lode, kill for fool's gold; later in the abandoned mine, the bureaucratic soul collapses, dazzled within transparent walls.

IN FOREIGN TONGUES

FREDERICK BUSCH

Let me make it clear: I have my work. The group is more of a *social* outlet for me. I am far from discontent. We were at the Beatrice Inn on 12th Street in New York, and we were making believe. Solly was pretending not to think about food, even though he studied his Fat Book. Ouida spoke of her mother-in-law in a manner suggesting that life on the same planet was feasible for them. Boris, whose son had quit a fine arts major at Skidmore to join the submarine service of the Navy, spoke about his boy as if he liked to. Maybe he did; I hated to hear him. I swore that his son was fascinating, though, and that Ouida's life was free of influence by the rise or fall of her mother-in-law's blood pressure, and that Solly—he looked a pound or two larger than when he'd begun his diet—struck me as fairly trim.

In other words, we were doing what we'd done for the hours just past: sitting in a group and, for the sake of mental health, confessing as truth what might be lies. We were the core of Peter—Petey, we called him—Pasternak's Wednesday night group therapy session. We were in our early middle age, and often sad. We sat on Petey's bean-bag chairs, all of them fire-engine red and filled with treacherous granules that gradually, as the hour passed, let us down and down and down, until we lay nearly flat, looking up at the pressed tin plates of Petey's ceiling more than over at each other, and talking about what we wanted to hide and maybe still were hiding, and goading each other to come out, come out, come out. And every

Wednesday, after Petey praised us, as if we had accomplished more than talk, we went to the Beatrice and we sat some more, and once more talked. We were afraid to stop, I think. I think we were all so lonely that we might have talked all night, each day, all *week,* if there had been anyone unselfish enough to listen to so much Solly, Ouida, Boris, and me besides myself and Solly, Ouida, and Boris.

The Beatrice was a short flight down from street level, and was always noisy and bright, never pretentious, and never unhappy. We went there for inspiration, I think, and for the shrimp—low in calories, Solly said, dipping his bread in the olive oil which they oozed—and the sense of its being a *family* restaurant, a place to which we belonged and a place which was ours.

So we were sitting after dinner, drinking coffee and sambucca, smoking cigarettes—Boris was once more swearing to quit—and in an instant of silence, the sort that always made me fear that someone might start to weep, Ouida said, "I had a remarkable student for the first time this morning."

Boris, predictably enough, asked, "Did you have him on the piano bench, or were you patient?"

Tall and slender Ouida, with her hair as ever in a honey-colored bun on the back of her head, said, "Don't worry. He was nowhere near as thrilling as you once were."

Solly blushed. I laughed the laugh I hate—a kind of horse's snicker—and said, "Could I be thrilling, once, Ouida?"

She looked at me and frowned. Her large ears seemed red with heat and drink, and her brown eyes grew hooded. "I think so. Yes."

I snickered again, then laughed like a human being, and Solly said, still blushing, "He tries, but he just can't talk about sex. It's what Petey said, you know?"

"You don't have to *talk* about sex," I snarled at all of them. "You can just *do* it."

"Oh, goodie," Ouida said. "When?"

"We're engaging in the most hostile damned repartee I've heard since maybe our first session," Boris said. "You realize that, people?"

Ouida said, "I was only trying to talk about a student. A *girl.* She's going to be a decent player, I think. I mean, she's serious. There's money, of course. Upper West Side—Central Park West someplace. High Eighties. Her father's in—entertainment. Uhm, television, actually. She's in the sixth grade, and she can think about music. And other things. That's what I wanted to tell you, so will you *listen?*"

As she spoke, Ouida was lining up anything she touched—clean silverware, uneaten crumbs of *risotto* in chicken liver fragments, little packets of artificial coffee sweetener. Solly was entering *scampi* in his Fat Book, a spiral notebook in which he wrote each morsel of intake, and its caloric value, for the perusal of his nutritionist, who weighed him every two weeks, and then scolded him, and took a hundred bucks. He said, "What?"

"Listen!"

"Yes," Boris said. He sought agreement in much, and especially with Ouida; he found very little, or none.

"This girl, Elizabeth Church, is doing the Czerny she's so proud of—actually, she ought to be—and she stops, she looks at me from out of all her pale skin and a storm of freckles, and she says, 'I always think that outward signs *can* tell inner tales. Do you?'

"I reply, I *stammer*, that I hadn't thought of it.

"She looks at me and says, 'Hmm. No. Well, it's not the sort of thing people talk about, I suppose. It's just that Daddy was talking about a script he had to read for homework.' She giggles, thank God, and sounds like a girl for a change, and she tells me her father brings home television scripts, things that people propose to make films of. He has to approve them. 'He had one that didn't have a lot of words in it,' she says. 'Mommy wondered how the people could tell what it was about. She said it sounded confusing. But Daddy said that outward signs *can* tell inner tales.' "

"Inward tales," I said to Ouida.

"You know the man?" she asked.

"No. Of course not. I would have said—just *inward*. That's all. It sounds better."

"Wait a minute," Solly said. "Ouida"—he pointed across the table at me—"was it one of *his?*"

"It had occurred to me," Ouida said.

"Not a chance. You *know* my scripts don't get produced," I said untruthfully. They hooted and booed and threw imprecations about self-pity. I told them, "You're painting me rich and successful so I pick up the check." I felt glad.

"But it's a wonderful question she asked," Boris said. "Outward signs and inner tales."

"In*ward*," Ouida said, mocking me.

"Well, either one," Solly said. "Of course."

"It's true?" Ouida asked him.

"*I* think so," Solly said. "Look at good movies. Good TV, even. *Books.* Or all those short stories where people just sort of talk very tersely and not a lot happens, but you know *some*thing's supposedly been said, something important, you know? And then the story's over and nobody knows what happened except self-control was exercised?"

"I should think of that as an argument *against*," Boris said.

Ouida said, "Yes. What about body heat? Doesn't an outward sign of something within—inward, darling—have to give off some human *warmth?*"

I said, "This is boring. Let's talk about ice hockey. Or even the New York Rangers."

Ouida said, "Why not talk about softboiled *eggs*, for God's sake?"

Solly said, "I want to talk about what Ouida said."

"I'll bet you do," Boris said.

"No, Boris. I want to on account of she's right. She's talking about me. Well, you know. Not the piano lesson part, you goof. You know what I mean. I mean—*look.*" Solly held his Fat Book up. It was yellow-tan and, once hardbound, now a flabby envelope of green-ruled pages. "I take this everywhere. You know it. It's on my bedside table. My cats take turns crowding their bodies onto it for warmth on cold mornings. I take it into the bathroom in case I inadvertently swallow *mouthwash.* When I'm making breakfast for me and the cats, I'm entering what I'm going to eat. I take it to work, of course. It sits on my desk. My supervisor sits on it when she needs to talk to me, the cat. She does it because all I can look at, I find, when she does that, is her skinny little ass, pressing down on it. She knows it too. And I'm always looking up the calories in my calorie-counter, and writing them down, planning my intake, *confessing* my intake—you know, all of you. You know what I do."

"You just did," Ouida said, patting his pudgy hand and making him blush.

He nodded. "I do it every day. All weekend, I eat and I write down what I eat. I write and I eat. On Monday, and every day of the business week, I sit at my machine and work with other people's numbers and accounts, but I'm also writing my own. I wonder which are true? Because I write down what I'm going to have for lunch, for example. One slice diet bread, forty calories. One stalk undercooked broccoli, ninety-four calories—that's a *big* stalk, by the way. Half a three-and-a-half-inch water bagel, seventy-seven calories. You get the idea."

"Yech," Ouida said. She dipped her finger into the congealing oil on Solly's plate and slowly sucked it off her finger. Solly blushed once more.

As if to fight hers with his own, Solly lifted his thick index finger into the air and made his point: "But I don't *eat* what I *write*. I go down to the Brazilian Coffee Shop, and I have black beans and rice in their sauce, five hundred calories. I have the duck at Quatorze: seven hundred, maybe a *thousand* calories. I mean, green peppercorn sauce? And then I go to see the nutritionist, and I stand there on his scales. I get *covered* with perspiration, and it isn't just the heat or being fat. It's shame." He looked at us as if he hadn't been saying something similar for months. His eyes were enormous and wet. His pause was so significant to him, dear man. And he said, lower, "Shame. So you go tell me inner signs and outward tales."

Ouida picked Solly's hand up and kissed it. I thought he would suffer a stroke. She held his hand and caressed its soft, hairy back as if it were one of his cats.

"Jesus, Solly," Boris said, "that's not so bad. We've all *told* you so."

"No," I said, "his point is the inner-outer thing, not badness."

"Both," Solly said. His voice came gently, as if he were afraid to move lest Ouida set him down.

"Well, it's understandable, Solly," Boris said. "What the hell. You think one way, you do something else, that's everybody in the world you're talking about, pretty much."

"But could you tell from his Fat Book," I asked Boris, "what's inside his gut?"

"I could tell what's on his *mind*," Boris said.

"Or maybe just what's on the page? Solly's more than just a Fat Book."

Solly's eyes were nearly closed. I expected to hear him purr.

"Well, that's *life,* dammit," Boris said. "That's all. You can't know everything about people by reading from the outside in."

"Elizabeth Church's father says you can," Ouida said.

"And Solly just proved that you can't," Boris answered.

"No," I said, "maybe Solly commented on the nature of the relationship between the inward and the outward. Instead of saying there isn't a relationship, maybe he helped to define one."

"Too complicated," Boris said. "Too abstract. Too hard."

Ouida said, "This, from the man whose son—"

"Don't start," Boris said.

"—comes home on leave from an atomic submarine—"

"I'm asking you not to," Boris said.

"—where he's in charge of listening to the whatchamacallit."

"Sonar," Solly crooned.

"Sonar," she continued. "He comes home, after listening for all those weeks to blips and bloops, not talking to anyone, just listening. He hears whales and *scampi,* for all we know, and masses of cold water. Am I right? Cold water gives an echo? And he *hears* all this. And then he comes home to Boris and Barbara's apartment—"

"We don't pay rent anymore. We bought it. You could at least call it a condo while you make me nauseous after dinner. After-dinner betrayal, anyone? Or will you stick with booze?"

"—and he spends his leave, when he's there with them, not talking. *He never, ever talks.*"

"He's tired," Solly said.

"It's possible he just isn't used to saying a lot because of his job, Boris. I did suggest this. You dismissed it," Ouida said.

"Well, I should have. I mean, I supply prosthetics to hospitals. I'm a *leading* supplier. You think I should go around limping? In a wheelchair? *What?*"

Ouida said to us, "He hasn't a leg to stand on." Solly laughed, silently, until his face was crimson and his chest was heaving. But Ouida had let go of his hand. He kept it on the table before her, as if it were part of her dessert, forgotten for now, but there for nibbling.

Boris didn't laugh. He wiped and wiped at his unstained mouth with a corner of his napkin. He finally said, "Not funny."

"We know it's a problem," I told him.

"From Mister Warmth, no less," he said. "Tell Barbara. She's the one starts crying as soon as he comes in."

Solly said, "Maybe that's why he doesn't talk."

Boris nodded. "I barely talk to her myself," he said from the corner of his very clean mouth. Then he said, "Joke."

We all nodded, and soon were silent and serious, tired, worried, I think, about the silence seeping in.

Boris said, "Not that much of a joke. He looks so—peaceful. He doesn't complain, he doesn't sulk. You talk to him, he smiles and answers happily. Gently. And then he crosses his legs and puts more chewing gum in his mouth and very sweetly sits there and looks at the wall across the living room. Barbara put a chair there, where we used to have a planter. So she could sit and watch his eyes and know when he was seeing her and wait for him to respond. But then she got hysterical when he didn't. 'You're turning me *invisible!*' she'd shriek. And he'd say, 'Huh? Excuse me, Ma?' and she'd go absolutely nuts. So I made her stop sitting there. Now nobody sits there. He comes home and he stares, and he smiles, he eats dinner with us and looks at TV, and he doesn't talk. I forget the name of his boat. I forget where the hell he sails in it. Whatever they do in submarines—do they call it sailing? Who knows? *I* don't. He doesn't tell us. Barbara's been bleaching her hair a very bright— really, a ghastly shade of blond."

Boris looked up. He'd been studying a line of matches laid down by Ouida. He wiped the corner of his mouth and folded his napkin on the littered tablecloth. "You think that's like your Fat Book, Solly?"

I asked, "How many calories in hair coloring?"

Ouida giggled and Solly, when he saw her reaction, smiled.

Boris said, "Beep. Beep. Beep. That's what he hears. Beep. Maybe it's all that he needs."

I said, "He interprets his world through the noises, Boris. He reads the world. Those are the signs the kid was talking about, her father, really, was talking about—the piano player?"

Boris said, "We did not raise our only child ever, in the history of our lives, to learn the world through earphones. Please *don't* tell me it's all right."

Ouida said, "I didn't mean to be cruel, really."

Boris said, "Oh, no."

"But maybe it's more satisfying to him. The electronic noise, the filtering-out of everything else."

Boris said, "More satisfying than we are, you think."

"Well," Ouida said.

Boris said, "Yes."

"I mean, I *understand,*" she said. "Don't forget—"

"We remember about you," Solly said.

"Dear man," Ouida said, but she didn't, to his patent disappointment, stroke his hand. "Don't forget that I am the only young—nearly young—widow I know whose mother-in-law is still offended by a marriage she hated. Even though it ended when Richie died, she insists on fealty from me—I mean, I *have* to feel sorry for her. And she does remember. No. She *knows.* She can tell me things about him I never suspected. I receive some of him that way. I always swear I won't, you know. I promise myself that I won't. That I will never see her again, or ask her to talk to me about him, or sit there to be insulted, demeaned. While she sneers at me because she cannot *bear* that I was me, not her, when we were married. It's like the Fat Book, Solly. I keep writing down that I won't ever eat that again, but I go out and I *dine.* I feel so horrible afterward."

Solly nodded and nodded, like something on an antique German clock.

"I'm so dutiful, I make myself sick," Ouida said. "I ride out there on the train to Harrison. I take a cab to her house. That maid admits me, the one who never talks. And I wait. I mean, I've *telephoned.* She's said, 'You'll have to come for tea.' It's like a horrible medicine one of us has to swallow. Both of us. And then I sit there, in a dark anteroom that always, always, always, always smells like wet raincoats. Even when the sun shines. And I try to read but I can't, because it's unlighted and I'm scared. As if I were waiting to play a recital!

"She has a room out there that the maid always shows me into. It's filled with uncomfortable chairs and all kinds of hairy plants—you can't see anything, some kind of fern or bush or little tree in a little pot or tall spindly chair with no cushions is always in the way. She sits there. She frowns at me. She pours me tea. She puts it on the table in front of her, and I have to come over from whatever slab of hard wood I'm sitting onto fetch it. We sit. She sips without making a sound. I, of course, always slurp. I can't help it—the tea's too hot. And then she talks. Only then. 'Well, how are *you*,' she always says. She's reminding me that I haven't asked about her, I suppose."

"No," Boris said. "That's the tone Barbara takes when he comes home. It's fear of disappointment."

"I will not be made guilty about this, Boris."

"It's only a suggestion," he said.

I asked, "Are we talking about the same outward signs that mean *different* inward things?"

"Inner," Solly said.

Ouida nodded. "Wouldn't that make life complicated? Not to mention stories like this one about it."

"Tell yours," I said. "And don't be guilty."

"I wasn't suggesting that anyone feel guilty," Boris said.

"I apologize for growling at you," Ouida said. "I have to protect myself."

"Not if you tell the story," I said.

"Clever," Ouida said.

Boris said, "I don't get it."

Ouida said, "So we sit and I slurp and then she beats me with good manners about the head and neck for a while. We talk a *teensy* while. And then—I can't help this—my head turns on my neck while my brains fall into my stomach. They keep shouting up, 'Don't turn! Don't *turn!*' But I look over at her little table. It's near a window box. She keeps—junk, I guess. Memorabilia, would you say? I don't know. It's like her horrible *mind*. She has all this stuff on it. Little Russian babushka dolls, one inside the other? A big set of them. Sometimes everything's inside the biggest one, sometimes they're all out. Sometimes one or two are out. And I keep trying to figure out what she *means!* There are nineteenth-century page cutters to be used on old books that she never uses them on, as far as I know. And paperweights from Italy that don't hold any paper down, and inside of the glass it looks like little *squids,* not anything lovely. And a very beautiful small ceramic watering jug with a crack, it looks like, running down the side. I suppose she pours water onto her jungle from it, if it doesn't leak all over. I've never seen her do it. And the Pennsylvania Dutch figurines."

"Oh," Solly said.

"I'm sorry. I can't help it. I can't even *believe* it."

"No, I wasn't complaining," Solly said. "I don't remember you ever talking about them before."

"Sure, she said," Boris said.

I shook my head. "Never."

Boris said, "Oh."

Solly nodded.

Ouida said to him, "So why did you say 'Oh'?"

"It sounded mysterious," he said.

"Oh, that's *sweet*," she told him. She patted his hand. He went nearly incandescent. "But I never talked about them?"

We all shook our heads.

"Well. Well, all right. I mean, we *are* talking about outer signs here. All right. So I look over, every time, and she sees me. She's watching. She sees me, and she starts in talking about Richie. How he didn't wear his snowsuit in the Blizzard of 1947 or something. And I really want to know that. I do. It's something to have. There *was* one in 1947 where they lived. Everybody stayed home, all the parents and the children, New York City closed *down*. Richie built a snow tunnel that went all the way across the street. They lived in Forest Hills, then. And he refused to wear his snowsuit. It was an adventure, he told her, and no adventurers *ever* wore anything *like* a snowsuit in any of the books that he'd been reading. He was always a terrific reader. So he went out in corduroys and black rubber galoshes—with those metal fasteners? He got sick. She thinks he got scarlet fever because of that. *I* think he got it from living with her. People *can* really get you sick, I believe. Oh, I'm—yes. Yes. I'm storing it up to keep for when I'm alone, but I'm also looking at her table. She has these figurines. They're made of cast iron, about four inches high, three-dimensional—statues, I'd guess you'd call them. Little Pennsylvania Dutch farm people. And they're always changed! She moves them around, depending on her mood. They have these painted-on dungarees and gingham shirts, and there's a Daddy and a Mommy and a little boy and a little girl. Their smiles are huge and empty. It's frightening. When Richie and I went to visit, the little children would be standing close to the parents, and we'd know it'd be all right for a few hours or a day. Or they'd be a couple of inches apart from the parents. Then we'd know she was hating me again for taking her son, whatever it was I did. Do. I don't know. And we'd make jokes about it when we were alone. But never with her. Because, one time, Richie asked her why she kept moving the figurines around that way—Richie wasn't ever frightened of anyone—and you want to know what she said? Not 'I don't.' And not 'I have my reasons.' Not 'I do?' or 'Do I?' or 'Huh?' She looked her son right in the eye, pausing only an instant so she could frown up through my eyeballs and into my brain, and she said, 'Which figurines do you mean?' "

"Perfect," I said. "Excuse me."

"No, you're right. It *was* perfect, it was so insane. Almost as crazy as my going to see her."

Solly said, "You don't want to *lose* him, Ouida."

She held his left hand with both of hers. He patted the knot of hands with his free hand, then kept it there.

"So I go there," she said, "and I do the tea, the slurp, the look, all of it. And I end up caring where she's put the silly cast-iron damned *statues*. Last time, the girl was lying down. Lying on her stomach on the table!"

"Voodoo," Boris said.

"Jewish voodoo," Ouida agreed.

I asked her, "Did you fall?"

"I worked so hard at making sure I didn't, you know, trip on the doorsill going out or something, I ended up falling into the cab and banging my shin. I cried all the way to the station. I hated myself. I *blamed* myself. *That's* Jewish voodoo. Solly, dear, my hands are hot."

"Oh!" he cried. "Geez! I'm *sorry*."

"No," she said, "not at all. I probably worry too much about my hands."

"Solly'll read a lot into that," Boris gloated.

But Solly, emboldened, looked up at Boris and said, in a very high-pitched voice, "Beep."

"So," I said, "how do we feel about Ouida's new pupil?"

"It *was* your script," Boris said.

I asked Ouida, "Was it about a father who pushed his son to play high-school football? Did the boy wreck his knee in a nasty accident on the playing field? Do we see the father, a month later, looking down at the leg of his sleeping son? Looking at the scars as if they're routes on a frightful map?"

"You did write it," Solly said. He smiled broadly. "Say, this is exciting."

Ouida said, "*I* don't know. She only talked to me about her Daddy and a script and what he said. I never read it."

"But you did write it. I can sense it. Right?" Boris asked.

"I don't have sons," I said. "I don't have daughters. Or wives. I don't write scripts about sons. I never wrote a script about a knee. Can you think of anything worse than a movie about knees? Or sons? Or wives?"

"A movie about cast-iron figurines," Ouida said.

"A movie about the sonar-operator on leave who never talks," Boris said.

"A movie about a Fat Book," Solly said.

It was ending. It was over. I nodded, accepting the return of my credit card from our waiter, and adding a handsome tip. We were ushered from our table with much courtesy, and we all uttered broken tourists' Italian as we left. *Buona sera,* we called, as if we lived where such a phrase were spoken. *Buona sera.*

And outside, adjusting clothes and hefting parcels and bags, we clung a moment more to our company, breathing dark Manhattan air, absorbing the sounds of cars and sirens, readying ourselves to cross Eighth Avenue or climb down into the subway or walk cross-town.

Ouida kissed us each on the cheek. She held the lapel of Solly's jacket and smiled to him. Boris and Solly and I shook hands. "Another week," Ouida called. "Another week."

Solly looked as though he'd weep. And so, really, did stern Boris. I wondered if I did too. Ouida looked happy and brave.

Boris moved hesitantly toward the corner where he crossed each week.

I said, "Don't wait. Goodnight, goodnight. See you at the session, Boris. Goodnight."

He nodded, and soon he stood at the curb.

Solly didn't know which way to walk. I told him. I said, "Solly, go home."

"Right," he said, turning toward Greenwich Avenue. "Right. I ought to feed the cats."

"Been a long day for them," I said.

"Solly, take care," Ouida said.

Solly uncertainly said, "Yes."

In her long, broad-shouldered melton coat, her cheeks flushed with drink and conversation, Ouida looked to me like the spirit of New York City in the winter. I belted my double-breasted trench-coat, and I pulled the buckle tight. "I think I'm gaining weight," I said. "All these dinners at the Beatrice."

Ouida put her hands above the belt, as if to feel my ribs. "Oh, I don't think so," she said. "But if you're worried, you can read a few pages in dear Solly's Fat Book. All of his pages are dietetic, you know." She kept her hands on my ribs. I put mine on her shoulders. "Do you ever feel lonely?" I asked her. "Besides missing Richie?"

Her smile moved my hands to my pockets. She moved hers too, but to gesture happily at the milky glow of Manhattan's evening sky, the bright, snarling confusion of its traffic. Across at Greenwich, Solly waved, a boy on the landing of the stairs at bedtime. I waved back.

Ouida said, "Well, this is the *city*. This is where people *always* sometimes feel lonely. Aren't we supposed to?" Now she waved goodnight to Solly too, and he went out of sight toward his cats. "Am I misunderstanding something?" she asked me.

Goodnight, Solly.

Goodnight, Boris.

Ouida. Goodnight, Goodnight. *Buona sera.*

"Nah."

WEIGHTS AND MEASURES

RICHARD SIEBURTH

BLASON DE LA TÊTE

(Version)

1. A head without dreams is a body with no grave.

2. A lifeless head, a head with no core : ripe for the sword.

3. Behead me : what is written in my skull cannot be earsed.

4. Cut off my sex : my pleasures are not disgraced.

5. A silver head deserves a desert rose.

6. Follow a madman's head and you will reach a river.

7. A bald woman thinks only of her comb.

8. Every crease in the skin, the death of kin.

9. The salt of the brow is the sugar of paradise.

10. Eyes are your measure : close them, and you are left with holes.

11.   However high the eye, the lash is always higher.

12.   The narrower the forehead, the more goatish in bed.

13.   A cock never crows on the same cheek twice.

14.   A fly lays no eggs in a cautious mouth.

15.   The blood of the lamb flows quicker than the tear.

16.   Where the tooth smiles, suspect treachery in the heart.

17.   His chin is long, his temper short.

18.   The tongue as sly in praise as in slander.

19.   Your nose is my black stone : I circle it seven times.

20.   Your brow is blacker than the owl on a white ridge of sand.

21.   Complexion so white neither wasp nor snake shall bite.

22.   Knead the lips with kisses : the night shall bake them into
                                                                loaves.

23.   Spatter her face with chicken blood ; now let her womb greet
                                                        the winter moon.

24.   Horses, not men, are judged by their nostrils.

25.   May your lips be the lids of the prophet's eye.

26.   A whore's spittle cannot slake my thirst.

27.   The jaws of a dog will never praise God.

28.   Wind in my ear, rainstorm in the throat.

29.   Though the sky sow broken teeth, face East.

THE ADAMS CABLE CODEX

Barthes in memoriam

Ailment,	—has been seriously ill, but is recovering, and—the doctor thinks will now do well.
Aimless,	—is better and we expect to leave here . . .
Albatross,	—is ill.
Aimlessly,	—is ill, but not seriously.
Alacrity,	—is ill. Case quite serious.
Alarum,	—is ill. No chance of recovery.
Albanian,	—is ill. Return at once.
Albino,	—is ill. Return at once. Do not delay.
Capacious,	Am alone.
Caparison,	Am alone. Meet me at . . .
Caper,	Am alone. Where can I meet you?
Caperling,	Am coming over.
Capias,	Am not coming over.
Capillary,	Am not coming over at present.
Capitation,	Am not quite . . .
Capitoline,	Am not quite sure,
Capitulate,	Am unable to . . .
Capote,	Am unable to decide.
Capricorn,	Am unable to decide what to do.
Capsicum,	Am very anxious to hear (about . . .)
Capsule,	Am very anxious to hear from . . .
Captious,	Am very anxious to hear from you.
Captivate,	An accident, not serious, has occurred.
Captive,	An accident, quite serious, has occurred.
Capture,	An accident, very serious, has occurred.
Capuchin,	And if you can . . .
Capulet,	And if you cannot . . .
Caput,	And perhaps not then.
Caracole,	And then . . .
Caramel,	Answer "yes" or "no".
Caress,	Are you going to remain where you are? And until when?

Caressing,	Are you ill?
Caribbean,	Are you ill? Telegraph reply.
Caricature,	Are you in need of . . .
Carking,	Are you in need of any assistance that I can render?
Carlock,	Are you in need of money?
Carmine,	Are you satisfied?
Cloven,	Come back at once.
Clown,	Come by . . .
Clownish,	Come here.
Clubbed,	Come here as soon as possible.
Clumsily,	Condition is improved.
Clumsiness,	Condition is unchanged.
Cluster,	Condition is worse.
Dictionary,	—is injured, but not seriously,
Dietary,	—is injured quite badly, but not fatally.
Diffidence,	—is injured dangerously.
Digestion,	It is too late?
Dignified,	Is it true?
Dignity,	—is missing. Have you seen or heard of him (her)?
Digression,	Is there any change?
Pelagien,	Accident very serious.
Pelagiorium,	Accident will probably prove fatal.
Pelagique,	Accident may or may not prove fatal.
Pelagonum,	Accident probably not serious; will keep you fully posted.
Pelagosaur,	Accident resulted fatally.
Pelamide,	Death was sudden.
Pelamydem,	Death was expected
Pelamydiss,	Death occurred at . . .
Pelamys, ·	Death occurred from . . .
Pelandola,	—died of . . .
Pelandusca,	—died suddenly.
Pelanibbi,	—died of heart failure.
Pelanoi,	—died of pneumonia.
Pelapolli,	—died of typhoid fever.
Pelaran,	—died in battle.
Pelargone,	—died in accident.

Pelattage,	Physicians hope for the best.
Pelauder,	Physicians hopeful.
Pelaza,	Physicians express some hope.
Pelazgas,	Physicians not very encouraging.
Peldano,	Physicians have given up all hope.
Rentage,	Have just learned of your illness.
Rentroll,	Have just learned of your marriage.
Reparation,	Have just learned the sad news.
Repartee,	Have met with a serious accident.
Repass,	Have met with a slight accident.
Repasture,	Hope all are well.
Requester,	I miss you very, very much.
Requiem,	I shall miss you very much.
Residuary,	Is quite ill, but doctor says there is no occasion for alarm.
Resignant,	Is rapidly sinking.
Resistive,	Let me know as soon as any change occurs.
Resorted,	Let me know everything.
Retrograde,	There is a slight change.
Retrospect,	There is a slight change for the better.
Retrovert,	There is a slight change for the worse.
Reunion,	There is no change.

FIVE POEMS

PETER READING

1
Cro-Magnon, simian, Neanderthal,
whom Mr. Justice Russell sentences
to 46 years (total) for assault
on Mr. Harry Tipple and his wife . . .

Charles Bradford, Terence Bradford, Edward Mitchell,
broke into Mr. Tipple's corner shop.
After they had assaulted him he had
black eyes, a broken nose, bruised lacerated
torso and face and buttocks. He had his head
banged on the floor and had his feet stamped on.
He was knocked senseless with a bottle. Cans
of aerosol paint and fly-spray were fizzed up
his nose and mouth. Bradford and Mitchell next
started to cut his ear off, but then hacked
off Tipple's toe with a serrated knife.
The toe was then stuffed into Tipple's mouth
(playing *This Little Piggy* on the kid's
little pink blobs is not so much fun now).

And Mrs. Tipple croodles in the box
as she explains how both her eyes were blacked,
her nose was broken, she was "in the most

humiliating and degrading way"
indecently assaulted by the men—
one of whom "used a knife in an obscene
bizarre vile filthy ithyphallic manner."
Charles Bradford, Terence Bradford, Edward Mitchell,
before they left the Tipples bound and gagged,
turned, faced them, and, unzipping, each produced
his member and pissed long and copiously
into the faces of the hapless pair,

An acned trio lowers from the front page.
Cro-Magnon, simian, Neanderthal
(but the same species as Christ, Einstein, Bach).

Trite impotent iambic journalese,
Reading Raps Raiders/Poet Pete Protests.]

2

Esther Albouy was twenty-one years old
when the war ended, and she was denounced,
by neighbours in her village in the Auvergne,
for fraternizing with a German soldier.
She had her head shaved in the Public Square.
Her parents, who were overcome with shame,
then locked her in her room, letting her out
only at night, occasionally, on a leash.
When, after twenty years, her parents died,
she could not bear to face the outside world.
No one had seen her go outside the house
for thirty-eight years.

1983:

some Carmelite nuns managed, at last, to get
an eviction order for a house they owned
where no rent had been paid for many years
by the occupants—an old woman recluse
and her two brothers.

The *Gendarmerie*
had to use gas masks when they forced their way
into the house, so overpowering was
the stench from filth and a green rotting corpse
(one of the brothers died three years before).
The gas and water had been long cut off.

She and her one surviving brother, whom
she slept in the same bed with, were removed
into a psychiatric hospital,
tenir en laisse, so she is pleased to think.

4
The Buffet carriage lurches side to side
causing a democratic crocodile
(*Financial Timeses, Suns,* a *TES,*
spinsterly, oil-rig drunk, a see-through blouse,
two Sikhs, a briefcased First Class parvenu)
to jig like salts on storm-tossed quarterdecks.
They're queuing up to be insulted by
a truculent steward who administers
flabby cool BR toast at wondrous cost
and steaming tea in polystyrene cups
capped with thin leaky plastic lids—the car
oscillates and an old unfortunate
is scalded by spilt pekoe and then hurled
onto the carriage floor, striking her head
hard on an angle of formica counter.
A cooling tower, scrap cars bashed into cubes,
a preternaturally mauve canal.
The cut is dabbed with tissue, pronounced "slight,"
a volunteer fetches another cup,
someone produces an Elastoplast.
A Long Life shudders towards the table edge,
cramped buttocks stiffen in an orange scoop
of ergonomic fiberglass. Cropped boys

aged about sixteen, manifest recruits
(numbers and names and barracks stencilled white
on khaki kit bags), smoke, guffaw and swig.
One of their number, as a furious shepherd
might bellow some remonstrance at his dog
when it is five fields off, recalcitrant,
brays "Ara sexy gerraknickersorf!."
(A teenage girl of average composition,
buying a cling-filmed slice of currant cake,
stimulates this encomiastic greeting.)
Their left hands grip their right biceps, whereon
their right forearms are raised and lowered. One
pustular soldier of the Queen pretends
to grapple with an imaginary huge
phallus—his fellow-warriors are seized
with mirthful paroxysms. They all have spots
(compulsorily shaved, not left to heal)
and all read comics—caricature army,
balloons of speech exploding from their heads:
"Chuck me that Sten, I'll get the dirty dastards."
Slight, acned raw cadets who may well be
spatchcocked in Ulster or some bloody fool
flag-waving bunkum like the Falklands do . . .
Company Sergeant Grit—Soldier of Stone,
Battling Burgess of the Fifty First,
Stens in the Jungle, "Get me them grenades,
I'll show the ruddy rats how us Brits fight" . . .
The peaceful fields are littered with new lambs
fattening up for Easter, SO_2,
pretty canary-yellow against grey,
sweals from stark plant (the voguish acid rain),
Long Lifes vibrate, totter towards the edge.

I edit Readers Writes (the Letters page):
"What has gone wrong with Britain since the War?,"
"Ex-Soldier, Telford" asks, "The Socialists

allowed the lower orders too much hope
by promising them radically improved
living conditions, and the dangerous
doctrine of lower-class participation—
the riff-raff started meddling in Power . . ."
"I blame the Immigrants," "Housewife" opines,
"for inner-city strifes . . . ," "The world's gone mad!,"
"Sir—Are we to assume that Western Powers
exercise no control upon their own
Military Forces? Murder has been done;
but if it suits a Military Élite
(under a Government's auspices or not)
no felon may be charged—an impotent
electorate sees its Judicature abused
by its elected leadership . . . ," "I heard,
distinctly, on the 4th of January,
the Cuckoo calling in St. James's Park . . ."
Of course you can't print half of them—obscene
or batty: "Mrs. Thatcher is a cunt"
(plenty like that, whichever PM's in),
"I'd bomb the fucking wogs," "Hanging's too good
for bastards like that" (muggers, hijackers,
people with beards, the unemployed, the child-
molesters, Hindus—everyone, it seems,
arouses someone's wrath), "Dying's too good
for vermin like this" [so we stay alive].

These are the days of the horrible headlines,
Bomb Blast Atrocity, Leak From Reactor,
Soccer Fans Run Amock, Middle East Blood Bath,
PC Knocks Prisoner's Eye Out In Charge Room.
Outside, the newsvendors ululate. Inside,
lovers seek refuge in succulent plump flesh,
booze themselves innocent of the whole shit-works.
Why has the gentleman fallen face-forward
into his buttered asparagus, Garçon?

He and his girlfriend have already drunk two
bottles of Bollinger and they were half-tight
when they arrived at the place half-an-hour since.
Waiters man-handle the gentleman upright,
aim him (with smirks at the lady) towards his
quails (which he misses and slumps in the gravy—
baying, the while, for "Encore du Savigny").
He is supplied with the Beaune, which he noses,
quaffs deeply, relishes . . . sinks to the gingham
where he reposes susurrantly. There is
'63 Sandeman fetched to revive him.
Chin on the Pont l'Evêque, elbow in ashtray,
as from the *Book of the Dead,* he produces
incomprehensible hieroglyphs, bidding
Access surrender the price of his coma
unto the restaurateur, kindly and patient.
These are the days of the **National Health Cuts,**
days of the end of the innocent liver;
they have to pay for it privately, who would seek anaesthetic.

CUTT'S GRACE

BRADFORD MORROW

> None dances whom no hate stirs,
> Who has not lost and loathed the loss.
> Who does not feel deprived.
> —Laura Riding, *After So Much Loss*

Still in the black suit he wore to the funeral and not five minutes in mother's house Cutts looked for, found, and pulled down on the cord that hung from the trap door to the attic. Georgia stood behind him, not dancing in place but shifting from foot to foot, black pumps off the way people in a family can do, that is, stand staring, barefoot—

Cutts, what are you doing? I said. Georgia, what's he doing?

—and Cutts climbed up the creaking ladder that dangled from a square in the ceiling like a tired lattice tongue, and as he did ignored both the women standing there in the hall. A dry mist of plaster dust was shaken into the hallway with each step he took. Georgia said he had better watch it, that thing was so rickety (meaning the ladder) that it looked like the whole apparatus was going to work free of its old bolts and come crashing. Cutts disappeared without a word into the square hole of the ceiling.

That's his way, Georgia said.

I got something in my eye; Georgia took me over to the window and told me to look up. She folded her handkerchief into a pointed cone and removed it, this particle fallen from the attic.

There, said Georgia.

She told me to wash my face with cold water: my eyes were

puffy from mother's funeral. We could hear Cutts walking around overhead. Muffled, dull, like a thunder miles away in a stale afternoon, the way it plays around the perimeters of a heat lightning. That's what his tramping around resembled. The thump of a chair, or perhaps a lamp, its globe chipped, its wire frayed, carried from upstairs with weight and overtone. Georgia had taken a brush out of her purse and combed her English-robin-breast-brown hair. But when will this water ever get cold? I wondered—

. . . and thought of the time I had been in England, with mother to visit her mother's sister, which was just an excuse to go there for once in our lives, which is what we did, and the thing I know she best remembered was seeing an English robin nesting in a sailor's hat for some reason stuck in a raingutter outside the window of the hotel where we stayed. That's another story . . .

Mother'd been dying for years, of a variety of ailments. I nursed her through the days that led from one problem to another; during these last twelve months, though, the pain made her behave peculiarly. Cutts, my brother, had brought his wife Georgia in September, all the way from Massachusetts, everything being a long way from Ohio at least partly because Pennsylvania's so long and boring and ugly on the road. Mother couldn't recognize either of them—Cutts, Georgia—and so she asked them to leave. Except for me, during this time I have in mind, she never recognized anyone; not the neighbors, some of whom she had known her whole life, not the minister, not even Dr. Fraley whose own father had delivered her wailing into the world in the same house that stands three doors down on the block. Fraley and Reverend Robotham'd each witnessed in their professions (can the ministry be called a profession, or is it strictly a vocation?) this kind of gradual lapse before, but Cutts took it hard (*Ephram, you get back home, or else*—

Something heavy dropped now above where I stood in the bathroom, the cool water cupped in my hands. Box of glass? of pewter? that cabriole-legged corner chair with the hideous beige upholstery . . . how blue, to my eye, how worn my hands have gotten, but—

—*Grace, show Ephram here to the door and point him in the right direction home, go on. And don't forget to latch that screen.*

But mother this isn't Ephram, it's Cutts.

Hey it's me—?

Cutts.

That's it. Cutts. Me, your son.

Cutts, she said again, pondering.

Right.

Get me some ginger ale.

And yet when Cutts returned to her bedroom with her glass of ginger ale, she sat up suddenly in bed, her hair undone, flying in spiky wisps: *I thought I told Ephram to get—and look here, he still is here? You little—go on, you get out of here.*

None of us knew any Ephram.

She's lost her mind, Cutts whispered in the front room. Fraley's a goddamn waste of money.

I had never noticed how the vessels could stand up so tall on my brother's forehead before, yellow-white as banana meat.

Cutts and I never saw each other after he and Georgia moved East from this town of Bergholz but I remembered that voice, that rasp; it trembled at the edge of his teeth. Georgia understood Cutts' voice, too.

Cutts, she said.

She'll outlive us all, and then he seemed to be finished talking about it.

In the front yard my (they were *mine* because *I* took care of them) gnarly crab apple trees were twirling their new leaves; so were the spring leaves in the birch, and the cherry.

Well, said Cutts, and backed away toward their car.

Well, so . . .

Georgia stepped forward and embraced me. Listen, Grace, anything you need, just write, or call, call collect. Cutts?

Cutts was already in the car; the luggage had never been taken out of the trunk, so I never got to see what brand it was. It was a good car, though, foreign. I don't know what kind.

Thank you, Georgia, I said.

You take care, darling.

She turned to go.

Oh, Georgia?

Yes.

She doesn't mean to be like that to Cutts. She's that way to everybody.

And they left, not to be heard from until I wired them—preferring cables to the telephone—about mother's death.).

During her last month she began to ask for Desmond in the night. She had never concealed her preference for Desmond over Cutts. Desmond had been her favorite, her final-born, her glory; upon him she pinned an entire gamut of hopes. Desmond undoubtedly would bring fortune and respect to their family, a world should spread before his feet malleable as warm bog loam and accept in its passive surface whatever stamp he might elect to impress upon it. But, for all the substantial qualities attributed him by his devoted mother, Grace and Cutts' younger brother Desmond was weak.

Lanky, proportioned like the reflection in a funhouse mirror, Desmond stood a head taller than any of the other boys he and Cutts had for friends. Gamely, he was seen to trail behind the pack, loping, slouched, knuckles swinging at his sides like a tight row of bantam eggs attached to the ends of his fists. Under the proprietary wing of his brother, Desmond pursued whatever follies the friends did, less for the adventure in and of itself than for Cutts' treasured attention. His wildness belied his weakness. He played willing fool whenever called upon to do so. If Cutts had his first toke of grass at eleven, did his first tiny theft, Desmond accordingly had and did his by nine. The tolls of Desmond's adolescence were an arithmetic function based on Cutts' own imperfections, needs, frenzies; Desmond himself wasn't compulsive, but was caught as if in a vacuum created in the wake of his brother's will. It was always just ahead of him, drawing him on.

Cutts knew it was for his approbation Desmond lived. He offered it only when he found it convenient or useful, when it fit into some specific scheme. If it suited Cutts, whenever any or all of them were in trouble, Desmond would be delivered up as the collective scapegoat. Out from under Cutts' fickle wing he would come, tacit and willing to atone for some petty theft, a watertower east of Bergholz painted with obscenities, a broken forearm, a separated shoulder, a split eyelid. In time Desmond had a worse reputation than Cutts, or any of the others. This is why when he broke this code of silence about what had happened to Grace that one August evening, sunk now with twenty-five others, no one listened to him.

After August Desmond got moody. He exiled himself from the

gang of boys. He disappeared days at a time, wouldn't speak when spoken to . . .—And he died (whether I like to admit it, it seems so impossible still) before his twentieth birthday. We would never be sure what finally had happened. There was no looped belt nailed to a basement crossbeam, nothing as simple as that, no bridge off which he hurled himself. He just tumbled down the stairs to the basement, opened his head on a flange where the railing had been detached. Cutts found him first. Grace had been putting out bread-crumbs on the crunchy snow for late robins and meadowlarks. A man named Beechel Gray, the butcher, took the call from Cutts and passed the telephone across the smooth pink stone counter to Desmond's mother.

The water, loosely cradled in my fingers, cooled my face. I soaked a hand towel under its thin lazy stream and, leaning forward over the shallow sink, while holding my hair up off my shoulder, ran the cold, wet towel across the nape of my neck. It trickled down my back when I stood up straight. I wrung the towel, folded it, replaced it on the rack.

Reflected in the mirror I was surprised to see Georgia leaning, arms crossed lightly, against the jamb in the doorway of the bath-room, looking at me with an expression indescribably—quizzical. Her oval face, pretty and punctuated by sharp features, whiter than the veiny marble of the sink, was set off by her black dress and heavy, dark hair—more auburn than even mother's had been. She smiled, lips tight. That better? I turned the water off. See, I knew that'd help.

She remained in the doorway as I brushed my hair. She seemed . . . what? . . . amorphous? central in my little scape, but some-how unreachable, immovable, as if lacquer clouded the short space there between us.

Didn't mean to startle you.

Oh—and the bone handle made a neat clack as it was put on the basin ledge. Is Cutts still up in the attic?

Yes, God knows what's so important he couldn't even change out of his suit before he had to go up there clambering around in all that dust and cobwebs.

. . . and Georgia made a sign for me to follow her, turned sud-denly, and walked down the hallway in the opposite direction of the attic ladder, to the kitchen at the back of the house. When she turned around again to face me, the color in her cheeks and neck had changed; she was flushed. In the haggard afternoon light whose summer skies were gathering thunderheads in stacks of white and violet and green-gray out all the windows, her lips had gone ashen.

Can we talk for a moment? she asked, quietly.

Is it about the house, because if it is I won't know what to say, Georgia. (Having literally forgotten her son's existence, mother willed me her house and possessions.)

No, no, something else completely.

Well.

Look, I know it's a bad time, terrible time, to talk about things, but since you, we never see you, and Cutts has got to be back to work day after tomorrow, I feel I have to talk to you now.

Georgia sat at the table in one of the highbacked cane chairs. The table was still cluttered with bottles of medicine, handwritten schedules for pill-giving and the administering of epsom baths, and on top of these pieces of paper a week of dishes I had not been able to bring myself to wash. Georgia fidgeted with a packet of cigarettes, drew one out, lighted it, inhaled profoundly.

About a year ago, I don't know how to say this, about a year ago, a little over, I got a letter. It was from your mother.

Oh? How Georgia thought it was possible for mother, invalided these past few years, who only came out into the sunlight when Robotham and I carried her down into the backyard and lay her on a clean blanket next to the bed of snapdragons and cornflowers, to have mailed her a letter I couldn't guess. I listened without questioning.

Since it was addressed to me, not Cutts, I opened it. It was the strangest thing. What was inside the envelope wasn't a letter from your mother—well, not a letter exactly, it was a kind of document, like a pact, I guess you could say, and all written out longhand on this oatmeal paper—? The *paper* traced an upwards arc, transformed itself into a question: Georgia hoped that I would by this detail—*oatmeal paper*—be prompted into recognition of something she'd rather not have to address herself, put into words herself.

I said, I see.

Well, the handwriting was a child's.

Cutts suddenly ceased his noisemaking. In a voice loud enough that it would carry upstairs, I asked Georgia: You like a little sherry? —I opened the cabinet door, got out two of mother's crystal vine-stemmed glasses and the Taylor's amontillado which was her favorite, so pale, so tobacco-yellow and strong, and brought them to the kitchen table. I could hear him at the farthermost corner of the attic, and then his silence again. I knew which barrel-topped trunk he was picking through now. It would take him half an hour to dissect its contents even if, as I suspect, he didn't bother to re-place what he'd removed.

It had to be years old, I knew, the way it almost came into pieces along where it was creased. Anyway, it was a pact—

The silence from Cutts' periphery unnerved me but I thought: —Go on, let it happen, whatever happens, let him come down now, let him do us all the . . .

—between Cutts and your brother and . . .

Desmond?

Yes, and some other names, too. They'd made this treaty. It was, well—but, Grace: I can't, well, what I want to ask is, is it true?

She had put the question to the reflective circular surface of sherry, stationary on the table before her.

Georgia, I'm sorry. I don't understand what is it you want?

She glanced up at me in disbelief, her forehead a patchwork.

I thought: —What a lovely woman. Worry can sometimes be so becoming in a person.

You mean you don't know?

This made me impatient, but just instantly, and it passed.

That attic where everything was lost. And father downstairs, se-dated. Dr. Fraley had gone home. Dr. Fraley had put his syringe, his morphine, his instruments, back into that black, scratched, and bubbled leather bag, and he'd gone home. Mother and me the doctor had left to stand by the bed to prop, reprop pillows, smooth the coverlet, gaze into his eyes clear and vacant as a monkey's in a zoo. Dad not knowing where he was, pushing up with his hands outstretched as if something up on the ceiling threatened him, push-ing and pushing it away. This strange farrago of sounds he would make so upset mother she left the room. The light in the room, color of a peach pit. Eisenhower talked Dulles-talk in his simple

way on the scratchy radio, and made Daddy happy. Evening.
August. Back when. Kitchen smells.

Desmond? mother on the other side of the door hollered. Dessie.
Then she returned, sat down on the bed, its springs complaining.
Go, would you, Grace, and find those brothers of yours.

I ran outside into the radiant twilight. Fireflies already glittered,
their green lamps stabbing the trees along the sidewalk. The drug-
gist's was empty, its row of stools with mottled leather cushions
aligned forlorn before the long counter, seltzer and Coke spigots,
ketchup bottles, salt shakers, the stainless steel malteds cup—

Not here . . . I know where they are.

—and all the movie posters I loved to start into while I sat up
at the counter sipping my cherry soda, especially the one for *Life-
boat,* all those courageous, desperate men and women huddled to-
gether, with the mad blue lithographed waves licking the prow of
their doomed boat, and as I stared into an image I myself would
easily slip inside, so that it was I who held in *The Red Pony* the
red pony's rein.

As I ran back along the uneven slabs of concrete I then knew
where Cutts, Des, and the gang were hiding. Cutts didn't want to
see him, Dad. Des would want whatever his brother wanted, no
doubt, but he, too, ventured into the bedroom only when mother
made him, to kiss his cancered father goodnight, or to say Good-
bye before taking the bus over to Akron to visit Uncle Tune.

The fireflies stood out more now, disposed to teasing the corn-
field and hovering in the light draught crossing the lawns. I got
back home, quietly entered by the side porch. Mother was still in
Daddy's room. She was reading aloud,

> . . . shall come forth a rod out of the stem of Jesse, and a Branch
> shall grow out of his roots, and the spirit . . .

in a singsong.

Once safely past the half-shut door, down the hallway, I groped
for the cord hidden in darkness and could already hear them stirring
upstairs in the attic. It was one of their sacred places. A crack of
yellow light, excited by shadows, thrown from a candle flame,
broke through to me when I pulled down releasing the ceiling
ladder. The silence that accompanied this broken pattern of light
seemed strange, and I had the sensation of being tipped upside

down and dropped into a dreamy, maybe unfriendly, Wonderland.

I climbed the ladder, eyes on each rung where foot over foot I placed my weight. I had never been up to the attic before. Why was it they were all so quiet? I wanted to look up but was afraid I'd lose my footing. I was too terrified to scream when hands and arms came down suddenly around my body and I was lifted away free into the pitch air, too shocked as my weight gave in, my legs kicking kicking, these strong strange fingers that hoisted me by my hair and my dress tight in under my neck just starting to tear and my legs and arms into the horrible with hands all over my down in but—

Someone whispered No, someone hit me.

Crazy old goddamn dead bitch. Jesus, what a pigsty. Sixty years with never so much as a tatty housecoat fed to the incinerator, never one single burned-out toaster tossed in the trash. Real hoarder. Here's a milk carton filled with plaster of Paris. Why? Here is a bird cage, cockatoos, canaries, we never had any, sight of a bird she'd be covered in hives.

Allergic to everything, so's sis, so was Des. And here this tittied mannequin, purse-lipped, bobbed nose, always a faithful mistress to us and how we loved her, so indulgent the little bitch, how many times did I? Little liver in the knurl and wham.

Trinka, stiff staunch goddess, nympho. Dressed her, undressed her. Real personality. Still has. Right now I could without half. Lighty with his heating pads, his magazines, his paraphernalia. Holy this place was for us, sacred and hallowed and one hell of a. Wonder did the old bitch ever wonder.

Watch out the joist. O bike, tires the rubber hard, flat. King of hearts, jack of spades, grandma's canasta cards still there on the rim, clothespins over the spokes ready to go snappety-snappety-snap.

Crazy kids! Mueller with his half-arm, how'd he lose it? Born that way, maybe. That little nipple on the end of the stump, murder at tetherball. Menace to the prudes, freakshow. Wonder who, what he's sticking it with right now. Might be pushing up roses, the Mule might. Skin white as a factory-fresh softball. Those red basset eyes blown straight down the pike from Mommy, that sad old show, real guzzler. Like a barn, that one was.

Me standing on the Mule's shoulders, hands loaded with thorns, moonless night, peeking in at her naked as an elephant, fold on endless fold of flesh, bottle in one hand and cigarette in the other, sunk back in that armchair watching the black-and-white set. No husband from the word go.

Poor bastard Mueller. There she was, always alone, always the curtains undrawn. Old sow must've known, might have put the Mule up to it.

Here's the photographs, won't look. The old man, won't look. So sour-smelling, not sweet like mothballs, but this paper, these books, the mildew.

Roof must leak. Somebody's nest, tickertape, little mouse. What we need here is a little sharp cheddar, a trap and ping! Who was it we made eat the mothball soaked in his own piddle? Phineas. Shaker Heights, lawyer now. Wouldn't his wife love to know about

Wake up, wake up, wake up, *wake up*.

Goddamn that little bitch . . . it's not as if . . . it's got to be here somewhere. It never happened that's what happened.

Dirty *little* bitch.

Why don't we leave him be, Grace advised Georgia. They had left the kitchen for the deep veranda that ran the entire length of the front. Two phoebes started, shot from their mud nest ledged in the rafters. The dense, earthy air had begun to move. Miles out to the horizon a black bank gusted eastward, diligently following the columns of rain that preceded it, released from its nearest edges. They could see the storm, through the vined screen at the west end of the porch, out over the plumes of big-leafed oaks and cottonwoods, as it descended toward them. The birds and cicadas were silent.

Feel how quick this heat is breaking.

But Georgia said nothing; she watched the inscrutable face— severe, childish, intent—and marveled at how few features Grace shared with Cutts.

It seemed to Georgia as if this face were wrapped in a transparent gauze, occlusively separated from the rest of the world, its desecrations, its filth. Grace forbore, was absorbed in the smallness of her own life, it seemed to Georgia. She rocked, lazing, in the porch swing.

Grace said finally: You have it?

Yes.

Let me see it, then.

Georgia set her glass on the wicker stand. She pulled the small square envelope from her blouse cuff, like a handkerchief. Here.

Grace sat with the folded bit of browned paper in her lap for a moment, leveled her eyes at Georgia, who sat again. She unfolded it, and read expressionlessly.

What we done with Grace was law, it began.

With decisive, nimble movements she then refolded the sheet and laid it on the swing beside her. What we done with Grace was law, low-voiced, like a cough.

Georgia could hear her own breathing. The answers to the questions she wanted to ask had already come through Grace's few movements and by the distant injunction, *What we done with Grace.* She felt she knew the answers, but had to pose the questions in any case. Grace? What was it?

Abrupt, disconcerting Grace laughed: It was their precinct, their holy little . . . well, wasn't it?

No; I mean, what happened?

—and as abruptly the laughter stopped.

Poor, ridiculous Georgia, please. What do you want from me? It was a lifetime ago.

But, what are those other names.

Jesus, she said, and her eyes ran the length of the raingutter. They all just, they all . . .

Down another block someone honked the horn of a car.

Cutts, he?

Grace's lips closed into a fine, straight line.

Desmond too?

No, not Desmond.

Rain like an appropriate titter began to report across the roof of the veranda, and in the grass and trees out before the house. Grace watched Georgia weep, dryly.

Now I always liked her, always will. Way she helped me clear mother's medicines, useless now without a patient, and to gather them up into a brown grocery sack, tie it with string and bury it under the other garbage in the tin can out in the alley so that none of the neighborhood children or any dogs could rummage it up. Way she set to washing the dishes, while I dried, both of us dressed in our mourning blacks, sleeves rolled up to the elbow. Way she had held me in her arms, rocking gently, as the porch swing creaked. Way she had let me take her by the hand and lead her out into the light rain, around the side of the house, where the hollyhock fell over itself in its own abundance, into the kitchen through the back porch. It was not a time to run into Cutts, was it? both of us in tears? and him in his rage at not finding it? And the way Georgia would never ask me whether it was I who sent the letter, and the way she would after all go back home with Cutts, because she felt assured that in the passage of time I had in fact forgiven him, and how she could feel this was true because it was I who insisted I had forgiven him . . .

But how the matter now would never come to rest inside her, how it would gnaw, how in the oddest instants it would come up, like a nausea, outrageous and insuppressible. How Cutts would never again be able to run his hands over her, push himself inside her. That was over now. And Georgia surely preferred knowing this truth about him. She would go on home with him, they would lie down at night after the long journey, but it won't be Georgia asleep beside him in their bed. Not truly Georgia.

She standing next to me before the sink. Her long delicate hands pushing the dishcloth around the stained circle of a plate, staring hard into the water. A real sister.

And all the while the noise Cutts makes upstairs growing more and more violent. His cursing filters down like a shower in a nightmare where the rain soaks its victim though never gets him actually wet—however drenched in his own sweat he may be on awakening in his twisted bedclothes. Poor Cutts, the way he would go on up there, looking and looking. Let him break every stick of furniture, every memento, every bit of family history in that badly lit, hysterical attic.

Let him shout; let him grind his teeth.

ELEVEN PROSE-POEMS

CHARLES SIMIC

1
The old farmer in overalls hanging from a barn
beam. The cows looking sideways. The old woman's kneeling
under his swaying feet in her Sunday black dress and touching the
ground with her forehead like a Mohammedan. Outside the sky is
full of sudsy clouds above an endless plowed field with no other
landmarks in view.

2
Things were not so black as somebody painted them.
There was a pretty child dressed in black and playing with
two black apples. It was either a girl dressed as a boy, or
a boy dressed as a girl. It had small white teeth. The
landscape outside its window had been blackened with a heavy
and coarse paint brush. It was very quiet except when it
stuck its little red tongue out.

3
He calls one dog Rimbaud and the other Hölderlin. They're
both mongrels. "The unexamined life is not worth living," is his

favorite saying. His wife looks like Delacroix's half-naked Liberty. She wears cowboys boots, picks dangerous-looking mushrooms in the forest. Tonight they will light tall candles and drink wine. At midnight they'll open the door for the dogs to come in and eat the scraps under the table. "Entrez, mes enfants!" he'll tell them bowing deeply.

4

My mother was a braid of black smoke.
She bore me swaddled over the burning cities.
The sky was a vast and windy place for a child to play.
We met many others who were just like us. They were trying to put their overcoats on with arms made of smoke.
The high heavens were full of little shrunken deaf ears instead of stars.

5

Margaret was copying a recipe for "saints roasted with onions" from an old cook book. The ten thousand sounds of the world were hushed so we could hear the scratching of her pen. The saint was asleep in the bedroom with a wet cloth over his eyes. Outside the window, the owner of the book sat in a flowering apple tree killing lice between his fingernails.

6

A poem about sitting on a New York rooftop on a chill autumn evening, drinking red wine, surrounded by tall buildings, the little kids running dangerously to the edge, the beautiful girl everyone's secretly in love with sitting by herself. She will die young but we don't know that. She has a hole in her black stocking, big toe

showing, toe painted red . . . And the skyscrapers . . . in the
failing light . . . like new Chaldeans, Pythonesses, Cassandras . . .
because of their many blind windows.

7

A week-long holiday in a glass paperweight bought at Coney
Island. The old lady wipes the dust every day. I call her "old lady,"
but she actually looks like a monkey when she peeks into the glass.
We wear no clothes, of course. I'm getting a fantastic tan and so
is my wife. At night there's a bit of light coming from the aquarium.
We turn green. My wife is a wild fern with voluptuously trembling
leaves. Otherwise, peace and calm.

8

My father loved the strange books of André Breton. He'd
raise the wineglass and toast those far-off evenings "when
butterflies formed a single uncut ribbon." Or we'd go out for
a piss in the back alley and he'd say, "Here are some binoculars
for blindfolded eyes." We lived in a rundown tenement that
smelled of old people and their pets.

"Hovering on the edge of the abyss, permeated with the
perfume of the forbidden," we'd take turns cutting the smoked
sausage on the table. "I love America," he'd tell us. We were
going to make a million some day manufacturing objects we had
seen in dreams that night.

9

Where ignorance is bliss, where one lies at night on
the bed of stupidity, where one prays on one's knees to an
especially foolish angel . . . Where one follows a numbskull to

war in an army of beatific dunces . . . Where the rooster crows
all day . . .
   The lovely emptyhead is singing the same snatch of a love
song over and over again. For breakfast on the terrace we are having
some eye-fooling painted grapes which even the birds are pecking.
And now the kisses . . . for which we forgot to remove our
Halloween masks.

10

   She's pressing me gently with a hot steam iron, or
she slips her hand inside me as if I were a sock that needed
mending. The thread she uses is like the trickle of my blood,
but the needle's sharpness is all her own.
   "You will ruin your eyes, Henrietta, in such bad
light," her mother warns. And she's right. The light gets grayer
and grayer. All our schoolboys are blind. Our winters last
sometimes a hundred years.

11

   It's a store that specializes in antique porcelain.
She goes around it with a finger on her lips. Pssst! We must
be quiet when we come near the tea cups. Not a breath allowed
near the sugar bowls. A teeny grain of dust has fallen on a wafer-
thin saucer. She makes an oh with her owlet-mouth. On her feet
she wears soft, thickly-padded slippers around which mice scurry.

SIX FRAXIOMS

ERNEST KROLL

DÉJA VU

If not
  Nihil in
this life,
check the
  Intellectu quod
dusty
back
  Non in sensu
numbers.

Tr.: "Nothing in mind but derives from the senses."

ROMANCE LANGUAGE

The lips for
  Parlez
French without
offense must
  Moi

pout in the
kissing
   D'amour
position.

Tr.: "Tell me, honey, what I want to hear."

VILLON

Young, you
   Tousjours vieil
pulled off
monkey
   Synge est
shines old
jockos
   Desplaisant
gagged at.

Tr.: "Old monkeys are always up to tricks."

ROMAN HANDS

A pinch and
   Les voyages
any frail
could hardly
   Forment la
fail to feel
she is a

Jeunesse
broad.

Tr.: "Travel shapes the young."

TRIVIAL PURSUIT

He ditched
  Vale puella
his flame
at the
  Iam Catullus
crossroads
hustling
  Obdurat
strangers.

Tr.: "So long, baby. From now on, Catullus goes it alone."

COLD SPELL

The cherry
  Was bleibet
in April
shivers in
  Stiften die
sleeves
of
  Dichter
bloom.

Tr.: "Poets establish the things that shall endure." (Hölderlin)

EXISTENTIALISTS

CAROL JANE BANGS

Grant wasn't the smartest of us—that was Brian, who by the third grade everyone knew was not just a teacher's pet but a genuine brain, so that no one was surprised when as a seventh grader he placed first in the state in the high-school math test and got to take classes at Morris College while he was still a sophomore. None of us were sure what he'd grow up to be—maybe a doctor like his father, or a philosopher or something—but we all knew he'd cut a wide swath in whatever direction he chose. And we knew most of us would be following different paths; we knew even then, even before the incident in the New York Y.M.C.A. and the hot pants at the high-school reunion and the custody fight over Elizabeth and his face in the newspaper two weeks ago, wasted and looking at death.

Brian was the smartest, even though I came so close on the math test that for years I thought the reason he didn't love me as much as I loved him was that he was intimidated by a girl who was almost as smart as he was. But we were all smart, Grant and Brian and David and me. We had been smart for so long we took it for granted and looked down our noses at the kids who got straight A's in home ec. or phys. ed. or regular English. We wanted to be intellectuals, to be like those two girls who graduated a year ahead of us wearing black turtlenecks instead of jewelneck sweaters, who had long dark hair and smoked cigarettes with long holders and smoked other stuff, too, the kids said, and who knew all about movies without subtitles and who made having sex in high school a political act instead of just something that your parents would die if they knew you were doing. We wanted to be intellectuals, like Camus and Sartre and the Bob Dylan of *Bringin' It All Back Home*. Brian was the smartest, but Grant was the most intellectual.

Grant lived with his mother, who was either divorced or widowed, though none of us were quite sure which, and who worked as a nurse, so she was often on the night shift and Grant had the house to himself. By the time he was a sophomore he was a good cook and kept up the house by himself. That didn't surprise us, because he was good at most things—even things we were supposed to look down on as "bourgeois," like water-skiing, snow-skiing, tennis, or dating prom queens. Somehow Grant could pull it all off—getting elected class president his junior year while taking classes in existentialism at night and, we suspected, sleeping with college girls he met over espresso at Portland coffeehouses long after curfew in the suburbs.

The night I sneaked out of my bedroom window to go hear Blind Lemon Jefferson, it was Grant who picked me up in his mother's beat-up black Volkswagen beetle. He'd turned the lights off so the neighbors wouldn't see him pull up under the breezeway at the elementary school. I'd managed to elude the neighbor's dog and was congratulating myself as I brushed grass clippings off my black tights, and it took me a minute to realize he was already there waiting, watching me in his rearview mirror. Like a dummy I was standing right under the schoolyard light. He didn't turn on the lights until we were halfway down the hill and headed toward the highway intersection. Then he spoke for the first time. He told me he liked my earrings. I don't remember what I said, only that I felt very stupid at that moment and wondered if I looked grown up enough for him to think about kissing me. The next week he invited me to hear Gabriel Marcel speak on Christian existentialism, but I was afraid and said no.

After we all left for college Back East, Grant was the first one to drop out. Brian was still at Dartmouth, would be until Christmas his sophomore year, when he would be gang-raped on a visit to New York and would drop out of college to join Vista. David was at Antioch, spending his work-semesters at a theater in Princeton where he was falling in love with a Jewish girl from Philadelphia and writing me long romantic letters with an undertone I took years to recognize as sexual frustration and longing. I don't know now exactly why I came back to Portland; maybe it was the dorm food, or the Ann Arbor winters. I had hardly been back a month when Grant called. I was living with my parents, too broke to live anywhere else, and he was living with his mother, just a few blocks away. Maybe, if I hadn't still been a virgin, something would have come of it. But by then I was hooked on David's letters and fancied myself in a state of spiritual readiness, saving myself for the mystical experience he promised with the help of long quotations from Rilke, the Bhagavad-Gita, and The Song of Solomon.

By the time David came back from Antioch, sporting a thick red beard and a heavy army-green overcoat, Grant was engaged to Cindy, the expectant mother of his child. Neither of them seemed very happy about it. But somehow pregnancy makes some people revert to a lot of ideas they thought they'd given up with wearing suits and ties. I think they guessed from the beginning that the marriage would be a disaster. But they hadn't counted on Laura's being premature, on the series of expensive treatments and operations and last-ditch attempts it took to keep her alive that first year. I used to tell David it was keeping her going that kept them going, at least as long as they did.

When Grant and Cindy finally split David and I had been married for a year. Neither of us had the nerve to break a mother's heart by living together, so we took the easy way out. We were all students at City College then, trying to finish the degrees we'd started Back East, living near the campus in run-down apartments, organizing tenant unions and recycling centers, day-care centers and peace vigils. One marriage more or less didn't mean much; it was the community that held us together. I took care of Laura evenings when Cindy was working in the chemistry lab, and sometimes Grant would come by to see us both. It almost felt as if we were the family those nights, sitting together on the mattress doubling as a sofa, watching old movies on a black-and-white TV someone's parents had declared surplus. Once, after Laura had fallen asleep, we almost made love, but the phone rang and I had to answer it, and then it was hard to look at each other straight and so he left early. I tried to read Cindy's *Scientific American;* it was the March issue, with an article about DNA with lots of diagrams I couldn't quite bring into focus.

David was working nights at the Art Museum as a janitor; it was about then he started doing drugs pretty heavily. If we'd known we only had another year together, maybe we'd have tried to change something, but we just let things slide. He'd been living with a woman from his TM class for six months before we got around to filing for divorce. A lot of things happened to us all over the next few years. Cindy and I got Ph.D.'s; David got remarried. Once Brian and Grant came to visit me in Salem, where I was teaching for a year, but it wasn't like old times at all. At our ten-year reunion Brian showed up wearing purple satin hot pants. He was living in a feminist house in NE Portland and had just adopted a newborn baby girl he was naming Elizabeth, after his mother. Within a year the baby's mother would demand custody and would win, but at the picnic on the banks of the Willamette they seemed happy enough. A lot of people were uncomfortable with Brian, but I guess there's some homophobia everywhere. For myself, I was relieved. Somehow, after all those years, it was nice to think it wasn't my fault after all.

Grant wasn't the smartest of us, but he had the most business sense—that's what my dad used to say, maybe because Grant was the only one of us who ever had a job in high school, though I never thought washing cars was much of a job. I guess it was that business sense that paid off for him, though, more than college or the classes in existentialism—or at least it seemed that way up until recently.

When he took over as manager of the food Co-Op some people had trouble with his changes—getting real produce cases, for instance, and starting to carry sushi mats and cotton towels as well as granola and organic carrots. Laura used to help out in the store, cutting cheese and folding paper bags. By the time she was ten she could even run a cash register, though she preferred to sit out front, talking to the customers. By then Cindy was teaching in France, so Laura and Grant lived together in an old house near the Co-Op. When he started his own store it was in a warehouse that had big rooms upstairs, so they lived above the store and it was Laura's job to sweep up. I only visited them there a few times, and mostly we talked about my students and David's new life in Seattle and Brian's gay-rights activities. I wasn't very happy, and I guess Grant saw that, but he figured it wasn't really his business. And he had problems of his own. At least that's what I thought. He had lots of women friends, but nothing really steady. He didn't seem to need anyone but Laura—she was enough for him. Even though the operations hadn't completely taken care of one eye, so that she had a hard time looking at anything or anyone directly, she was a rather pretty little girl, right on the edge of adolescence, just "ready to burst," as my grandpa used to say. She liked me, or at least I wanted her to, so I would sit down and talk with her whenever I came by. We'd talk about boys and boats and her kittens, which numbered between three and ten, depending on how successful she was with her constant notices on telephone poles around the neighborhood: "Organic Cats—Free to Good Homes."

The summer I filled in for old Professor Enright at City College I went back to stay with my parents. Grant and Laura had me over for dinner several times, and since I didn't have a car and had to take the bus into the city, they would bring me home. The car was a convertible, some sort of sports model—I don't pay much attention to that sort of thing. But I remember how good the air smelled on those summer nights and how quiet and strange the world seemed when Grant turned off the motor at the beginning of the long slope down into the county park and we coasted for over a mile, nothing breaking the night but the wind in the trees and the sounds of animals in the woods above the creek. He fired up the engine just as we rounded the bend into civilization, the shopping center built where we used to play softball, the new senior center.

The house was dark when we pulled up into the driveway. Laura was asleep under a blanket in the back seat. Grant stopped the motor, and for a long time we just sat there, not saying anything. Then he pulled me over and kissed me—first hard, then soft, then on my cheeks, my eyelids, my neck. For a few moments we pulled together, letting ourselves be moved by those feelings we'd both known for years were there. But then the question marks appeared just ahead in the story. I gathered up my jacket and purse and let myself out of the car without saying goodbye. Because part of me wasn't leaving, I guess; because I knew I had to leave anyway. Because I was afraid of all we had missed, all that we could have had but didn't for all those years, and I couldn't help but think that after so much putting off of the obvious it was now too late. Laura was stirring, her head pushing around under the blanket looking for the edge, then appearing suddenly, hair tousled, to ask "Where are we?" and be told.

People tell me I'm very smart. They use clichés like "Superwoman" and "Type A Personality" to justify not really liking me very much. They tease me about always having the right answers and doing everything perfectly. I guess I can't blame them. I've got the degrees, the publications, the certificates and awards. I even got a blue ribbon at the County Fair for my jalepeño pepper jelly. I'm listed in all the *Who's Who's* that try to sell you leather-bound copies for your "personal library." But I don't feel smart at all. Maybe it just doesn't matter anymore. Brian was the smartest, but they took away his baby and he's dying of some disease we'd never heard of back then. David's third wife just had a baby, but he still carries the *I Ching* in his briefcase and isn't sure what will turn up. Grant was smart, but he didn't know that when Laura hiked up her first mountain she would get caught in a storm and die in a snow cave, two weeks shy of her fifteenth birthday, leaving him alone. Still, he was smarter than me. Even now I'm saying I couldn't have made things different, trying to believe that's true.

SPRING LOVE NOISE AND ALL

DAVID ANTIN

(*for ellie*)

                         i ran into austin gallagher on the way
to the bookstore and he told me some friends were putting
 together a reading in the grove celebrating spring and
love   and i guess i looked a little doubtful because doug
  rothschild called me a few days later to remind me that
 we were going to have a reading on the themes of love and
noise   but when i got here i found out that jean luc nancy
  had heard that we were celebrating love and laws and gave
a reading from plato   and doug told me he had said "love
and loss"   so i thought i was right in the first place
  and i would talk about spring and love and noise
                                              but i
wondered what i would talk about because here in southern
  california youre never really sure when spring begins i
mean the experience of spring
                              the vernal equinox is one thing
but spring is something else and ive been living out here
  twenty years and i cant always tell when its spring

          my guess is it comes on some time in late february
and you hardly notice it   a few branch ends turn yellow
  a few wildflowers begin to sprout   an occasionally

77

different bird appears   and you figure it might as well
  be spring
          now thats a little different from the kinds of
spring i remember where i came from
                  in the east when its
  spring boy are you ready for it   if you lived in new
york or upstate new york about 130 miles north of the city
  the way you'd know spring was coming was that around the
end of march you'd hear rolls of thunder or cannonades that
  would mean the ice was breaking on the river   you'd say
gee it must be spring the ice is breaking on the river
    and it was like a series of deep distant drum rolls
     brrrrrrrrrrrmbrrrrrrrrrrrm   and you didn't feel much
better about it because the sky was still gray and cold and
  the trees were still bare

      in fact you felt better in january   because the snow
seemed to keep you warm   especially when the temperature
 got down around zero and the snow was piled up around the
house and along the roadside   because after every snow
  the snow ploughs would clear out the road and pile up the
snow along the roadside into a wall from six to ten feet
  high   that would shield the houses from the wind   and
you'd shovel out a pathway to the street but inside it was
  warm   and pretty much everybody in this little town of
north branch felt insulated and warm and pretty good in
  january as long as the heating fuel held out   and they
didnt feel too bad in february either

       but when the spring came   in march   and you
    heard the dull cannonade on the river   thats
  when you started to feel bad   because it had been so
cold and bare and gray   and you had been holding out so
  long for the wild mustard and the goldfinches   and maybe
the coming of the quince   that the sound coming off
  the river   that seemed to promise an entry into the land
  of the hearts desire   which you knew would take another
month at least   made you feel real bad
     so thats why when the spring came to north branch at

   the end of march   it seemed that every year two
people would hang themselves off their back porch   because
   they couldnt wait anymore

                 but there was the other side of spring and you
expected great things of it   because you had read all
   those marvelous sweet and jingling poems by those
provençal bullshitters waiting for spring to come so they
   could go out into the fields and fuck and kill people
       brash and noisy poems that went on as i remember
something like "oh spring is here the birds are singing lets
   go out and fight some battles and make it in the grass" in a
cheerful jingling and very overrated way
                                         that my friend paul
   blackburn did the best he could with   which was to bury
   the jingle and jazz up the noise a bit   to make them
sound a little bit like ezra pound and a little bit like
   paul doing an east village macho number   and a lot
better than they sound to my ears in provençal   and with
   poetic generosity he covered up the banality of their
vocabulary and their tedious ideas if you could call their
   attitudes ideas and it all sounded so cheerful that we
thought it must have been a good idea to sit in toulouse and
   welcome in the spring
                     but dont you believe it   toulouse is a dreadful
place and nobody wants to be there   everyone in toulouse
   would rather be in paris   so if you have a choice about the
spring you dont want to spend it in toulouse
   paul actually lived there for a while   and he was
always running off to paris or mallorca or to spain

                but wherever you are you are likely to have this
   idea of what it means for spring to come   and you know
how it will come and when it will come   because in your
expectations it always comes   in a neat order the way
   seasons do   because there are exactly four of them
and they are very nicely named and there are exactly three
   months in them and they very obediently follow the
astronomical year

i once figured out a system for the southern california
year   i dont know if anyone understands it   but i once
  sat down and figured it out nothing about this climate
seemed to follow the pattern of my orderly astronomical year
          not its weather its seasons or even the variations
within a single california day
                              so i sat down and worked it
out   at least to my own satisfaction   for the stretch
  of coast extending from tijuana to santa barbara   i
dont know anything about monterey or oakland or san
francisco   but i think i think i understand the coast
  of southern california   at least from santa barbara to
the mexican border
                        the key to it is the afternoon   a warm
and luminous sunlit afternoon   all year long there is
  some point in the day   however short   maybe only an
hour that is filled with warm sunlight
                                          in the middle of
  december this might be only an hour somewhere between two
and three   and maybe its a little pallid and not
  quite so warm as the beginning of a sunlit morning some
time in summer   but its there   even at the winter
  solstice   if nothing else intervenes   like a
  little fog or rain   but thats an intervention i'll
talk about later because in principle the sun is always
there even in the dead of winter

              now as the days get longer this point of sunlight
expands   gets brighter warmer and lasts longer   and
  what we have is an expanding afternoon   that lasts at
first one hour then an hour and a half and maybe two
      until by what we call summer   its expanded to engulf
  almost the entire day   and then it starts to contract
again growing slowly and progressively shorter and cooler
through the autumnal equinox   shrinking to the same bright
  point at the winter solstice from which it starts again
        and because there are three dimensions to this afternoon
      brightness heat and temporal duration   i think of this
sunlit substance im calling afternoon as a kind of solid

which because it expands and contracts continuously and
simultaneously along all three dimensions   i see as a
kind of luminous warm cone   or more precisely as an
unending series of connected cones lying flat along the
continuum of time   a kind of brancusi "endless column"
lying down

now it doesnt really feel like this or not
completely   there are periodic and minor interruptions
like rain or cloudy skies that temporarily obscure the
pure periodic perfection of this expanding and contracting
luminous cone   and theyre bunched in clusters

the rain
almost all of it comes in what we conventionally call
november and december   or sometimes january or february
but the key to grasping this is to realize that it all
comes bunched in two or three day clusters   that disappear
and reveal the ongoing and constantly growing or shrinking
sunlit afternoon   there is also the overcast of june or
sometimes may   a thick cloud cover that for a long time
continues to obscure the true climate   but this too i see
as merely a longer interruption   to understand this all
you have to do is get on a plane   and climb a few hundred
feet to see that the serious business of the sunlight has
never been interrupted

now there are a few other
facts ive neglected to mention   the santa anna   a
sirocco-like wind blowing off the mountains toward the
water that establishes a hotter drier moment for a week or
even two   this can occur almost any time of the year but
seems most often in winter   now this intervention makes
any section of the cone seem hotter longer and brighter
but this is also an illusion   that is merely a
coupling effect that by burning off the cloud cover earlier
and keeping it off longer simply reveals the full extent
and heat of whatever segment of the sunlit cone is then
present
so you see the weather of california is a simple
and even monotonous business   beautiful as it is

but monotonous as all beautiful things must be   an
unendingly ongoing expanding and contracting cone of
   sunlight   randomly or maybe not so randomly   but
 arbitrarily intersected by brief invasions of rain or
cloud or santa annas and there are no seasons at all
  only expansions and contractions of an afternoon that
generate this continuously shrinking and expanding cone of
  light and heat in which theres nothing to wait for but the
brief invasions of the rain and fog and desert wind

               but in new york you really had something to wait
for   you knew you had three months coming that would be
   pretty much the same   and then things would change
     maybe for the better   and thats why you waited for
spring because things were going to be neat   you'd have a
  neat spring   and neat is the right word for it because
its very much like the ideas surrounding the spring
                                      we had a
quince tree once   it was actually a quince tree outside a
  house that we were renting from a local dairy farmer   and
when the spring came it began to blossom with beautiful red
   flowers   so that you thought of the spring as holding
out a promise of these bright red flowers   but in all
  those springs i only saw it flower once   because with
spring the buds began to open and a sudden frost would come
  that killed all the flowers   and as long as i was up
there we never did get any quince
                                 which was a little like
the black and brown striped caterpillars that also came out
  in spring   but i remember a sunny warm october an indian
  summer that some of these little jerks came out thinking it
was spring   crawling around and probably expecting in
   their infinite innocence to be turned into colorful
butterflies   and were turned by the cold into furry little
    black and brown caterpillar corpses instead
        and there was a certain murderousness in this   as
this second spring came out to clobber all those little
  bastards before they got a chance to fuck   as my friend
ted berrigan might have said

because that seemed to matter a
lot to ted   although maybe no more than the pills or
pepsi that finally took ted away so much too soon   though
   i dont know whether it was spring or not   but it
   felt awfully grim when i heard he'd gone away   and ted
was cheerful enough to be his own spring but even he couldn't
   hold up against the weather

        so thinking about the arrangement of spring and
its perfect organization   and then thinking of what spring
   means as an original heating up of the system   and of
how as a system heats up it gets noisier and things start to
   buzz around less controllably and bump into other things
      and how some of these collisions may be joyful and some
of them seem like theyre going to be more joyful than they
   turn out to be
                        i thought about one spring when i was
looking forward to good things   i was living in greenwich
   village on a one block street in one of those comfortable
little apartments that was so cheap i could pay the rent
with half a day's work   it was old and small
                  and it was on the fifth floor of a walkup
   that was built so long ago it had slave quarters in the
back   and i had to share a bathroom with my neighbor
   across the floor   but it had three rooms gas heat and a
fireplace and i could see the hudson and the palisades from
   my living room window i could smell fresh bread from the
italian bakery across the street and it only cost me
   eighteen dollars and seventy-five cents a month   which
included a rent raise of 15% over the last tenant   and the
   woman i shared the bathroom with was someone i was having an
intricate relationship with
                        she was a very attractive blond soprano a
coloratura who was struggling with her upper register
   which wasnt light or bright enough because her middle and
lower registers were dark and lustrous   and maybe she
   wasnt a true coloratura after all but her voice teacher
swore she was   and she was struggling with this   and
   also i think with being a mormon a jack mormon or lapsed

mormon who didnt go to church and wasn't living the kind of
    life she was supposed to live   and i suppose she was
struggling with this   and there was our relationship
    which was at intervals passionate and stormy and probably
not doing her a lot of good with all her other troubles
        but it was the springtime when people come out of
their apartments and begin to hang around the park where the
trees are flowering and old guys playing checkers and bocci

                    and it was the kind of particularly mild spring
that comes to new york once every four or five years   the
    kind i remembered as a kid with sunny showers drying warmly
on your shirt and carrying maple flowers in small rivulets
    down the curb   and this year it brought out a crop of
homeless people   the reagan government didnt invent
    homelessness they merely perfected it   but these were
mostly kids who'd left parental jails in ohio or indiana to
    look for real life on the streets of the big city   and
this spring they were camping out
                                a number of them had
found out there were a lot of flat roofs in the village and a
    lot of people who didnt care if they slept up there as long
as they didnt hold too many parties or make too much noise
    so they would stash their bedrolls up at the top of the
stairs above the top floor of one of the walkups a few
buildings down from where they slept to be less conspicuous
    and keep them out of the rain   i lived on the top floor
and i'd noticed   these two guys and a girl who i supposed
    were living on a rooftop somewhere down the block   and
one sunday morning i was going down to get the times and
    pick up some fresh baked bread and cheese   because this
was the week that according to ugo her teacher ruth had
found her upper register and we were going to have a
    celebratory breakfast   and i was halfway down the block
        across from cino's and not far from the bleecker street
boys club   when i was stopped by a crowd of people
    gathered around two cop cars that had parked in the
middle of the road   one of the cops had the blankets and

bedrolls and was on the radio   and in the back of the
car was the girl   a skinny teenager in jeans and military
jacket with a pretty face blotched from crying   i figured
someone had finally blown the whistle on our roof dwellers
      last night's party must have been too loud   and the
cops were busting them while all my italian neighbors were
standing around talking looking and pointing at the girl and
up into a building on my side of the street   out of
which two other cops pushed one of the two boys   a sullen
dark haired kid with pock marks into the back of the other
car
      the conversation was in sicilian but the gist of it now
came clear   a very old sicilian lady looking up at the
roof explained it to the woman from zampieri's
      "he wanted to marry her and she refused him and he was
going to jump off the roof"

      meditating on this excess of passion i wandered off to
the park instead of the cheese store   where i ran into a
friend of mine i hadn't seen in over a year   we got to
talking and into a chess game   that was eccentric and
complicated and lasted almost an hour   so that when i got
home ruth was angry and suspicious   i told her about the
police bust and the imaginary suicide threat   and about
running into gene and the game of chess   but she didnt
seem to understand   she said she didnt believe me that i
was making it all up and that i'd slipped out to go fucking
somebody else   and she began screaming and throwing things
and almost hit her cat rasputin who ran under the couch to
hide   and i apologized for a while till i got tired of
it and got mad and started yelling back till i got tired of
that and all the noise and screaming and breaking things
and went back to my apartment across the hall where i sat
looking out at the flowering sycamore in front of the
bakery smoldering and reflecting on the uncertainties of
spring till i heard a knock at the door and figured it
was time to go make up   but it wasn't ruth
            outside the door was another friend   and she had

a bottle of champagne in one hand and a jar of caviar in the
   other   she looked up at me with laughing eyes held up the
caviar and pointed toward the couch
               "its spring   i thought we might celebrate"
   and i took a good look at my friend   her beautiful sexy
little body her great lovely eyes her funny freckles on one
side of her nose and her slightly overfull mouth to make
sure that i wasn't dreaming just because it was spring
         and as we sat on my couch and talked i thought about
   how nice this would all be and how simple   and i thought
of my serious quarrel and my complicated relationship with
   my hysterical friend across the hall   i put my friend's
caviar back in the bag put the champagne bottle back in her
hand kissed her on the nose pushed her gently out the door
and explained we would have to take this up some time later
         and i did the serious thing   i went back to my quarrel
and my complicated relation with my hysterical friend
      which i believe ended three weeks later

         so much for spring

NEW MOVEMENTS IN EUROPEAN CULTURE

GEORGE STEINER

The two World Wars were *European civil wars.* They came to involve other continents and civilizations. But they sprang from within the dynamics of European nationalist rivalries and European ideologies. An estimated seventy million human beings were done to death by open warfare, political and racial massacre, deportation or starvation in Europe and western Russia between 1914 and 1945. These were European deaths within the material and psychological facts of European history.

The doctrines or pseudodoctrines of nineteenth- and early twentieth-century chauvinism, of Marxism-Leninism, of Fascism, and of National Socialism were, again, European. Their distant roots may, notably in the case of chiliastic Bolshevism and of National-Socialist Jew-hatred, lie in the late antique and medieval worlds. But their twentieth-century realization, both in blueprint and execution, was of modern Europe's nightmare and making. Auschwitz and the Gulag, the systematic incineration from the air of great cities, evolved from inside the politics, the technologies, and the vocabularies of European culture.

I have tried to show that there are connections, far beyond individual or temporal coincidence, between that culture, even at its highest, and the programing and performance of the inhuman. Important strands in European high literacy, aesthetics, and philosophic radicalism or nihilism not only underwrote certain impulses towards barbarism; they rendered European sensibility more apt to yield to the seductions of final savagery on the one hand and of self-deceiving inertia on the other. The shadow which now lies on the notion of culture itself, on the assumption older than Pericles, that literacy, humanistic education, and the arts humanize the individual and his society, is of the dark of Europe.

To ask about current and possibly new movements in European thought is, first of all, to pose the questions of Europe's engagement with its immediate past and with America.

The economic, the physical renascence of Europe after 1945 was, very largely, initiated and sustained by American generosity, a generosity singularly profound whatever the strategic, cautionary complications of certain of its motives. Europe has flourished materially while leaving to the United States the essence of its self-defense. Yet almost from 1945 on, European thought and self-consciousness have largely failed to come to terms with the American presence (a Raymond Aron was an illustrious exception). Much of European daily life, of the European urban environment, of European mass-consumption and the media, is by now thoroughly Americanized. A partially fictive "California" haunts the imaginings, the gait, the idiom of European youth from Oporto to Leningrad, from Stockholm to Messina. The best of America, however, does not export easily. It is a second-, a third-rate America which now asphalts European cities and dirties an ancient landscape with supermarkets and fast-food stands.

Correspondingly, a kind of sour, self-scorning anti-Americanism is a growing force (or weakness) in European psychology. It is almost the badge of a certain shop-worn social élite and of the *intelligentsia*. What is not visible is any serious endeavor to think through, to come to honest grips with, the condition of European identity and spiritual production in what has been, for almost half a century, an era of global Americanization. The very possibility that this era may now be ebbing, that a hemispheric or Pacific-oriented change in American commitments and interests may leave Europe to its own needs, makes an analysis, a clear view of American-European relations both on the philosophical and pragmatic planes the more urgent.

The continuing absence of such a view—it would entail a rather harsh look at the mirror—is debilitating. The European incapacity to face the tragic past and to experience uncompromisingly the intimate connections between this past and the tenor of the present, is even graver. It is not Germany, East or West, which alone has refused to confront openly, without moral or intellectual compromise, the recent European record of torture and holocaust, of despotism and mass-destruction. It is not only Austria, albeit that the Austrian amnesia is the most unctuous and flagrant, which has swept under the carpet the literal ash of yesterday. It is Europe as a whole. The psychic and political manipulations whereby the collapse of high European culture and of the legacy of the Enlightenment into homicidal bestiality have been forgotten or have been marginalized by being made the object of principally theoretical and academic debate, have been awesomely successful. *Hitler, ne connais pas,* as French teenagers replied to inquiring sociologists.

It has been argued that such suppression of unendurable remembrance and insight is necessary if an individual or a community is to recuperate its life-force. Whether this is so dubious. Plainly, the price paid for such evasion is steep. The triviality, the academicism which inhabit so much of recent and contemporary European creative and philosophic existence, are inseparable from some kind of "black hole" at the center. Less than fifty years ago, tens of thousands of men, women, and children were being tormented and made ready for unspeakable death each and every day within a busride. of that night's Mozart recital in Munich or Kant lecture in Weimar. This is where any thinking, feeling European must begin if he seeks some commerce of integrity and clear-sightedness with his own inheritance and future. Certain European thinkers and writers and artists have, indeed, striven to face, to give intelligible expressive forms to, this overwhelming issue. Their condition, in the culture of the tranquilizer, has not been easy. Such great witnesses as Paul Celan and Primo Levi have chosen suicide. Martin Heidegger stayed (damnably) silent.

Strikingly, much in the long-suppressed enigma of European self-slaughter and genocide is, today, beginning to hammer at our doors. The passionate controversy which has erupted among German historians and thinkers about the true relations between the world of the death-camps and the German national-political past, between Hitlerism on the one hand and Stalinism on the other, is symptomatic. Very tentatively, one would want to say that certain priorities of awareness are today changing in the European climate, that the shocks of recognition are beginning to be felt. Here again, an American withdrawal from European circumstances (however ominous on the political or strategic plane), could be salutary. It is the house of its own being that Europe must put in order.

The dominance of French literary-intellectual movements in the European (and trans-Atlantic) energies of discourse over the past four decades was grounded in the catastrophe of two European wars, of the German occupation of France, and of the Marxist-Stalinist challenge to the survival of European middle-class enterprise. Existentialism, in its Sartrian vein, is an attempt at a fitfully humanistic variant on the ontology of Heidegger (*L'Etre et le néant* being an extended footnote, a footnote humanized and psychologized by Jaspers, to *Sein und Zeit*). Camus's stoicism in the face of the absurd looked back to European warfare, to the concentration camps, and to Kafka. Derridean deconstruction is founded on Nietzsche and, more exactly, on Heidegger's readings of Nietzsche. Lacan's version of psychoanalysis claims a privileged fidelity to Freud precisely as Althusser's antihumanistic materialism claims to be rescuing Marx from misprision. There is an ironic sense in which these various and influential movements do represent a continuation of the German occupation of Paris.

Other motions of spirit and of method have a more native provenance. Paradoxically, perhaps, it is Michelet who is the begetter of the *Annales* school of structural and social-anthropological historicism. Structural anthropology itself, on the other hand, has been the most ecumenical of French exports. After Mauss and Lévi-Strauss it has looked back to the structural linguistics of Saussure and Jakobson and interacted, in complicated but fruitful ways, with the great Anglo-American lineage of anthropology and ethnography.

A macabre succession of deaths and personal misfortunes has befallen the high mandarinate of Paris. Of the seminal figures, only Derrida remains active (though, increasingly, self-denying). The methodological-rhetorical legacy of these several "orderings in France" now exercises a mesmeric fascination over epigones in Britain and the United States. Within France, the doctrines, the idiom represented by existentialism, by Barthes, Foucault, Lacan, Althusser, are now fading. On the German side, Habermas has subjected the philosophy of power embodied in Sartre, in Foucault, in the deconstructionists, to a vehement, revisionary critique. Habermas sees in these movements the fatality of the Heideggerian inheritance and of its solipsistic obsessions. It is with social, communitarian liberalism along Anglo-American lines, it is with a kind of "Atlantic pragmatism" of shared discourse, that Habermas would negotiate the new pacts of common sense.

Such a reaction is altogether sane. But the critiques of meaning, the radicalization of classical models of consciousness and society, the quest for "grammatologies" (which are, in fact, masked ontologies) of both the individual imagination and the social-temporal institutions which this imagination classifies and responds to, do represent a major moment in European moral and intellectual history. Habermas's critique is humane and bracing, but philosophically unpersuasive. The shibboleth of "shared discourse," of "face-to-face communication" (here Habermas's critique coincides with the religious-metaphysical meditations, today highly influential throughout the Continent, of Emmanuel Lévinas), will not dispel the presence of Nietzsche, of Heidegger or, one suspects, of Foucault.

Britain's long, and so far as general and journalistic literacy go, continued resistance to these dominant currents and debates, a resistance put up in the name of outraged good sense and of the dreary routines of logical positivism, can be seen as part of a much larger retrenchment. The domain of the humanistic in which, in Britain, there has been no retrenchment but, on the contrary, creative prodigality and quality of the first strength, is that of music. Not since the sixteenth and early seventeenth centuries has British music matched the quality and influences of that composed by Britten, by Tippett, by such current masters as Maxwell Davies and Birtwhistle. The relations between musical excellence such as Britain has known since the end of the war and the surrounding intellectual and spiritual ambience, is, at any given time and place, elusive, perhaps indirect. But we need only to look at the writings of Adorno—one of the truly representative figures in Europe's unresolved connections to America, in the problematic fabric of the European academic revival—to grasp its importance. It is, I believe, more than plausible that in the inward energies of recognition and rejoicing (Barthes's *jouissance*) of educated, feeling European men and women today the reception, the understanding of music is focal. Like chess—the two *are* related, but *how?*—music represents a brilliant success story in thought and imagining in post-1945 Britain.

A third pivot of European self-scrutiny and performative experiment has been, continues to be, that of Italian literature. Far too little known abroad (far too little read, if evidence is reliable, at home), the fiction of Gadda and of Sciascia, the poetry of Ungaretti, Quasimodo, and Montale, have conjoined classical narration and mimesis with the fragmentation of new, post-Joycean, post-Kafkaesque manners of feeling. In current Italian writing, films, even music, moreover, the truths of massacre and of civil war, of exile and terrorism, are vital. This *verismo* in regard to Europe's most recent past gives a special, somber luster to the severely academic, even philological criticism and scholarship of the two finest readers produced by mid-twentieth-century European culture. I am referring to Gianfranco Contini, whose linguistic-critical studies of French and Italian poetry, ranging from the Troubadours to Valéry and Montale, have gained classic stature; and to S. Timpanaro, who is at once a classical philologist of A. E. Housman's stamp, and a Marxist heretic who has produced inspired readings of Leopardi and of Freud. More generally, my guess would be that the locale, the context of values and forms in which the tension between America and European ideals, between a moribund Marxism on the one hand and the aspirations of a new social democracy on the other, will prove most inventive is that of northern Italy. It is in Milan, in Turin, that the genius of Europe strikes one as most hopeful.

No such hope mitigates the intense, almost hallucinatory art of Ingeborg Bachmann, of Peter Handke, and of Thomas Bernhard. Marginalized by the mendacity of Austrian life, these writers seek to give to the scarcely bearable claims of remembrance, of retribution, a legitimate function in Europe's present economic carnival (has the odor of money ever been stronger, be it in London or in Frankfurt, in Brussels or Geneva?). To those who can stomach his black fables of hatred, Thomas Bernhard is today the master remembrancer. His prose is, with Beckett's, that of an "afterword." Why, asks Bernhard, ought the native ground of the death-camps and the armaments brokers have the right to use the future tense? To which Spain, once Austria's partner in the *imperium* of Latinity and of European Christian centrality, would answer: because miracles of rebirth *do* occur, because languages and cultures, infected by forty years of Fascism and lies, can spring back to moral and artistic vitality. Look at us.

Any summary mapping will get things wrong. The omission of the exact and the applied sciences from a consideration of European intellectual, formative conditions in the late 1980s is an evident absurdity. To cite the obvious example: until very recently, Britain's decline and provincialization have been concomitant with something like world primacy in certain branches of cosmology, molecular biology, and biophysics. By definition, furthermore, the "Europe" I have been referring to is a crippled artifice.

There is no, there can be no meaningful concept of "the European" in the absence of Weimar, of Dresden, of Warsaw, of Prague, of Budapest and, cardinally, of Leningrad. The iron curtain may have been imposed and maintained by superpowers extraterritorial to Europe, but it is Europe's identity and future that are enfeebled. Perforce, it is poetry, fiction, music, and philosophical investigation from the east which speak most nakedly to our twilit circumstance. A good deal has been made available, at least via adaptation and translation, to the Western reader and audience. But far more remains clandestine or linguistically inaccessible. The decisive question we must ask ourselves regarding the reality and future of the idea of Europe has little to do with the bureaucracy and technocratic greed of the Common Market. It is this: will the very recent (tactical?) steps towards fresh air, towards some acknowledgment of truths, in Soviet internal policies, in turn, allow a freer commerce of ideas, of shaping expectations, between Eastern and Western Europe? Will the once-crucial densities of mutual awareness that knit Vienna to Prague and Budapest, that obtained between Paris and Leningrad, be reconstituted? But even if a new "openness" were to prevail, it is by no means certain that such densities can be restored on a continent which, through its eradication of the Jew, has deprived itself of the foremost couriers and antennae in the life of the mind and of the arts.

Doubtless, it is a banality to characterize the present-day tenor of European intellectual and aesthetic trends (itself a vacuous term) as "transitional." The notion does, however, have its application. The dilemma of America-Europe remains unresolved. The murdering past, be it that of the hecatombs of 1916–17 or of 1940–45, remains, to use the telling German epithet, "unmastered." The bankruptcy of Marxism has been that of the modulation of an analytic method and messianic promise into pragmatic practice. This bankruptcy has left a vacuum. Communist pressure was a stimulating goad; it helped provoke much of the most resilient, educative responses in postwar Italy and France. Now the cadaver of the old high dreams rots.

Many would assert the same of European Christendom. The febrile materialism—where "immanence" is the more exact word—of the European cultural climate, the nihilistic dispersal of traditional modes, can be read as manifest signals of the more or less tortuous end of religion. We come after Feuerbach and Marx, after Nietzsche and Freud. Most sociologists would concur; as, even more emphatically, would logical positivists and the very great majority of scientists and technologists.

I wonder. If, when future historians of intellect and of literature come to assess Europe in the mid-twentieth century, they seek to designate what proved endurable in intensity and quality of felt expressive life, they will find that religious inference, both explicit and internalized, has been eminent. The poets who will last, such as Rilke, Pasternak, Mandelstam, Akhmatova, Char, T. S. Eliot, Montale, Celan, are in constant dialogue with the metaphysical precisely at the point where it reaches into dialogue with God. The pressure of God's absence, where that absence is a mocking plenitude, informs the works of Beckett. Already now it is perfectly clear that both Heidegger and Wittgenstein labored towards the crucial demarcation between the immanent and the transcendent. Derrida's postulate that the intelligibility of semantic signs, an intelligibility which deconstruction fundamentally queries, is underwritten by the assumption of a "real presence," is a piece of negative theology in the most demanding sense.

But the theology produced in the age of European tragedy is far more than negative. It is, together with certain existentialist thinkers and artists, the theologians who have sought to situate the *mysterium tremendum* of ungoverned slaughter, be it in the trenches, in the burnt cities, in the death-camps, within the purlieus of intelligibility. It is the Cambridge and Aberdeen philosophical theologian Donald MacKinnon, whose *Theological Explorations* and *Themes in Theology* seem to reach deepest into the human, spiritual significance of what he calls the "sombre splendour and enormity" of the Leninist project and legacy. A sketch, however brief, of the best that is being thought and written in Europe which would omit, say, Lubac, Karl Rahner, Urs von Balthasar, would be a gross distortion. Asked to name the most acute inquirer into the meanings of meaning, into the *auctoritas* or hiddenness of tradition and textuality in European culture after the wars, it is not Roland Barthes I would choose first; it is Karl Barth.

The vitality of the religious in our poetics, the sheer distinction of the theological element in the European *genius loci* of today (here, also, Anglicanism is the gray, diffident guest at the banquet), does not, necessarily, entail any genuine religious revival. The churches may remain empty and the gulf between approved literacy and religious feeling may grow even wider. Christianity, in the vein of Athens and Jerusalem, of Rome and Reformation, may not resuscitate in time to stem the onrush of Islamic fundamentalism, or to face effectively the mushrooming of pseudoreligions, infantile cults and superstitions from East and West. Scientology, astrology, transcendental meditation, psychoanalysis may well be the satyr chorus bearing to parodistic burial the remains of the dead God.

The possibility of a reversal can, however, not be ruled out. Malraux's prediction that the coming era for man would be religious or that it would not be, may prove accurate. In any look at the current and nearing atmosphere of discourse and sentiment in Europe, the life-force of the religious is the most intriguing (seriously intriguing) of unknowns.

Signal anniversaries lie ahead: 1988 will see the celebrations of the nine hundredth anniversary of the University of Bologna. Considering the visitations of despotism and ruin on that luminous city, from the Middle Ages to 1944–45, what grips the imagination is a sense of the obstinacy of excellence, of the fertility of remembrance in the face of recurrent desolation. July 1989 will find countless men and women in pilgrimage to the Place de la Bastille to commemorate what Charles James Fox called the greatest day in the history of mankind. These commemorations of both constancy and Revolution should recall Europe to intimations of its special responsibilities for what has been at once preeminent and most fatal on the planet.

Responding to the terrors of 1916, to the collapse into murderousness of European and Russian civility, Akhmatova wrote: "For answer I hide my face in my hands . . . / but I have run out of tears and excuses." If Europe is to come to terms with this century and with its potential, this stance sounds just about right.

ELEVEN POEMS

RÜDIGER KREMER

Translated from the German by Breon Mitchell

1

the heroes
die lost
in the drifting sands
in pain
remembering
how chopin
leaned
smiling
against the closed grand piano

2

the children
sense trouble
first
frightened

by the sudden summer rain
and fearful
when the thrush falls silent
understanding
suddenly
what it is that waits for them

3

the travelers
endure travel
with difficulty
bearing up under
the heat of the day
beneath straw hats
awaiting
the cool of the evening
and relief
from their longing
for a sleep without dreams

4

the young women
lie barefoot
in the grassgreen grass
and look at
domed cities beneath the clouds
the windows of the little palaces
gleam in the light and in
the tree-lined lanes
they can see
the end of summers

5

the generals
in their open cars
keep dreaming and dreaming
of a better world
of a good world without people

6

the dead
are the friends that outlive us
on late summer afternoons
they climb over
the railings of the park
and in the evening dusk
without being asked
they scramble up
the lattice of the balconies
and through the french doors
consoling
with silent gestures
our deep desire to die

7

the idiots
sit in the garden
in early summer days
beneath the golden trees
they have opened
their collarless shirts
at the chest

swaying back and forth
in the wicker chairs
they laugh aloud
at every
thoughtless word

8 nachlass for R.

at any rate a biography
has to have something about death
even
if people don't die
quite so simply these days
of a gangrened leg
in a charity ward in Marseilles
or struck down
by a falling branch
in Paris
but at least one would like
to drown
on a diving expedition
off the aegean islands for preference
or even caught
by the rising tide
while strolling along the sand flats
off cuxhaven
just please not
in a plane wreck
on a cheap flight to mallorca

9 envy for A.P.

simple as taking notes it would be
with eyes closed

whiteblind
fingers would move
across the keys
no longer seeking
strange words
and even the weak
ringfinger of the left hand
would cease dancing out of step
would stop its foolishness
and all the lines
would choose themselves
would crumble
stealthily
into poems
insidious as tangos
as rapid as sad

10 westerholzstrasse for B.M.

i live in a quiet house
on a quiet street
twice a week
at eleven on the dot
they pick up the garbage
the postman seldom rings
for c.o.d.'s
court orders
registered mail
and letters with postage due
at noon the kids next door
come back from school
and furtively
throw tinfoil wrappers into my garden
in the afternoon
an old woman takes her son
out cautiously for a walk

in wind and rain
they walk together
like man and wife
and yet are mother and child
at twilight
the evening jet
roars by low in flight
passing over my house toward berlin

11 gas heat for N.

just a year ago now
i sat at this table
before the window
writing in my overcoat
like hardenberg
about how cold
accelerates the precipitation of ideas
now thermostats maintain
a warmth here
that makes me easy prey
to dreams
of wondrous poetry
and unexpectedly
i am assailed
by words that rhyme

TWO POEMS

ANTHONY ROBBINS

THEORIES OF DECLINE

Elsewhere the ventriloquistic gourd, ingredient of the oracular
succotash; the chapped persimmon, flagrant pumpkin later,
or earlier, someplace other than the disquisitional
mind, the mind's parfaited countryside of hyaline
and haydust; later the din of cutter-bar and bailer,
pandemonium of burning muscle. But here, within, under
the shadowy texture of the live green forever
oak, enscriptured with gray-green scalps,
with its bromeliaceous drapery of moss, hereunder
the blackforms of one-lobed leaves, the black
flitting bird-forms, under the obscure natural
ciphers coming between the sun and the imagining
eclipsed, or the man without, farthest from thee, out
where stars are the keen puncturings
of asterisks battering from inside the shell of the eternal
eightball . . . or here, here by the stinking lake
while we look at the lilies, white, partaking of the endless
effluent, leukorrheic flakes of a decomposing moon; here
beside the funny turtles, plesiosaurian, but with their shells,
    so shy,
climbing out of the dark silt onto the cypress
roots one upon the other in the manner of the English

poetic tradition, into the old starshine; here, now
the warm gulf sigh withdraws us, gently, toward our essential
shiver. Today
        the cape of autumn has fallen;
                    and the compulsion
to sing is thwarted and deepened by having had to read "la chair
    est triste, hélas."
Hélas, a mild nausea. Hélas, a locked jaw, iambic alexandrines
    leaking out
of the corner of the mouth, a dribble of gore, rank,
from the rank gullet of a heavy omnivore; Descent: Refrain: Falling
is so many things: black shadow of lobes scything
the surface of veins that warm in waves the back
of the white hand, cooling the surfacing blood, slowing
the circuit, enthralling the heart: is the earth's sickening
careen into darkness sung in the killdeer's urgency, felt

in the dream of a woman with a bag, gathering, in the slanting sun.
While elsewhere, higher, later, eariler, ice returns the oozing
prairie around the river's source to its essence: wolf-womb,
pike-purse, vortex of teal. The man feels
this, distantly, and the same ice drops in a drear (traditional)
(phalangial) tap on his shoulder, coldly, and upon the bruised,
    disquisitional
fruit of his mind, which, in lieu of the absolute
zero, or or the locus of the natural
falling or of the kind of autumn of his original
wounding, assumes the color of failure,
of desiccation, the color of earthenware,
of muscadine, dark and veiled degrees. Meanwhile,
elsewhere, outside the tree of his mind, his wife
gathers up warm pecans from the patio. Their child, in her
    perpetual
expedition, staggers through the weeds
holding overhead a sprig of dead oak, a flame
of brown dessicate leaves.

IT

is not here either, in the blue-blackness. Nor is the moon.
But say, "There are stars, a myriad." Say,
"My-ri-ad: the stars." And then there is a fulfilling
sensation of the picayune. Who are you? A drop perked out
from between the night's eyelids? The anthropomorphic wept?
And where have you had to step or have you been thrown out?
      Chart.
Near a coast that you might describe with the belittling phrase,
                              "Where they are
fighting it out," except that that is not nearly an inkling
      of where
you felt you were as the door clanked, the lever
dropped.
              And you stood here blinking at the darkness,
which advances, at the darkness, which recedes. It is so quiet.
Blinking above you is one bright star. Find it. Say, "Would
      I were
steadfast as you," but think again: having once more sent
yourself into a desert, or having come again to bay at the end
of a sea, having arisen when the wind is dead and the world
has stopped breathing, thought alone moves in the cold universe.
Think of the difficult pause of your being. Think of nothing.
We are definitely capable. We have made this dimension—only
                      for ourselves.

EVERY HOME SHOULD HAVE
A CEDAR CHEST

CARMEL BIRD

Lay up for yourself treasure in heaven, where neither moth nor rust doth corrupt.

The larvae of the cosmopolitan clothes moth attack wool, hair, silk, carpets, feathers, furs, and dried skins.

Clothing and fur insurance are what you buy when you invest in a cedar chest—a safe, moth-proof storage space, beautiful as well as practical. The moths that you see flying around do no damage; it is the young moth worms, deposited as eggs in dark and concealed places, that destroy clothing. The United States Government Department of Agriculture has definitely ascertained that cedar chests have a pronounced killing effect on moth worms. It is recommended that in using a cedar chest for the protection of clothing, fabric, and furs, special care should be taken to prevent undue escape of the aroma. The chests should remain tightly closed as much as possible.

Every home should have a cedar chest.

Furnish your home with one of these splendid cedar chests.

A chest that breathes of romance, with its suggestion of pirates' treasure trove. Made of genuine red cedar from the forests of California, furnished in natural cedar color, with a coating of genuine Duco. Neatly ornamented with 2-inch copper bands, studded with round copperhead nails. Easy rolling casters. Equipped with substantial lock and key.

Puerto Rican hand-embroidered costume slips possess a distinctive individuality. Fine enough for the most fastidious woman and lovely enough for the daintiest trousseau, this step-in slip of silk crepe de Chine is topped with dainty and fine quality lace and insertion, and is finished with lace edging. The embroidered net medallion and the lace insertion and the clusters of pintucks add an elaborate touch.

Peach, white, black, purple.

For the trim figure in fashion's favor, you will want these lovely high-grade rayon-and-silk jersey knit bloomers. They have the clinging softness of real silk, yet are made full and roomy. Have reinforced double fabric gusset crotch, elastic waist, and pretty lace-edged ruffle at elastic knees. Launder beautifully in soap suds.

Here you will find comfortable, scientifically designed brassieres for practically every type of figure. Brassieres should conform to the natural outlines of the figure—their chief purpose is to hold flesh immovable, not to compress it into much smaller space than it naturally occupies. The too tight brassiere affords one of the quickest possible means of spoiling the lines of the figure. Do not spoil, but improve or preserve those youthful lines. It will be to your advantage to follow our instructions "How to measure": Straighten back and shoulders; place tape measure around body under arms; pull smoothly, not too tight over fullest part of bust and give actual measurement in inches. If your bust measurement is 35 inches, order size 36; all brassieres are made in even sizes only.

Peach, white, flesh, orchid.

This long brassiere is specially designed for stylish trim figure lines.

Made of firm cotton with fancy silk elastic insets in the sides. Special stay-flat boning in front effectively controls the diaphragm.

Peach, white, flesh, orchid, rose.

Goats belong to the family of hollow-horned ruminants and are of the genus *Capra*, closely allied to the sheep. The goat has long been used as a source of milk, cheese, mohair, and meat, and its skin has been valued as a source of leather.

Europe's best offering of fine quality kid gloves made of real kid skins with the popular petit-point embroidered turnover cuffs.

Handsomely embroidered backs.

Black, gray, beaver, champagne.

Match your gloves with our special dog and wolf fur collar and cuff sets.

The eastern red cedar of America is much used in cabinet-making. With its suggestion of pirates' treasure trove.

Lay up for yourself treasure in heaven.

To be smartly dressed, you must be correctly corseted. Stylehint: Shape your figure into slim lines of beauty by wearing the lovely Pliant-B.

The baleen whales are distinguished from others by the possession of a double series of triangular horny plates anchored to the roof of the mouth. The inner side of these is frayed out into a fringe of bristles. The fringes combine to form a matted sieve or strainer for collecting the planktonic animals on which baleen whales depend for nourishment. It is these bristles, known as whalebone, which are used in corsets.

Shape your figure into slim lines of beauty by wearing lovely Pliant-B.

Lower part in front and at sides of back is shaped like a girdle and is cleverly fashioned of various sections of one-piece elastic. It hugs the body ever so comfortably, thereby subtly bringing out the feminine line. Fastens with a broad-end clasp at direct body center. The front panel of fine rayon fabric cares for the bust and fits neatly over the lower part, giving a flat front and longer figure lines. The elastic along the entire bottom edge cups the figure snugly, giving trim hip lines, and it expands comfortably when seated. Moderately boned with genuine whalebone. Six large suspenders. Creates a stylish contour, supports the abdomen in its proper position, reduces the hips and abdominal girth, and does away with the pushing of flesh into unsightly bulges, and the compression of the diaphragm. Can be laundered freely without injury. Lacing at sides and bottom front permits wonderful adjustment. Bends with the body.

Available in: peach, white, flesh.

The common silkworm is native to China. The food of its caterpillars is the leaves of the mulberry tree. The silk produced in the cocoons is of the highest quality, and highly sought-after.

Natural, brown, platinum gray.

And for a very effective appearance on the garment, add one of our squirrel-belly fur trims.

Beige-tan, mink-brown, platinum-gray.

The larvae of the cosmopolitan clothes moth attack wool, hair, silks, carpets, feathers, furs, and dried skins.

The wood of the cedar is decay-resistant and insect-repellant. Every home should have a cedar chest.

Cedar is the name applied to a variety of trees, both gymnosperms and angiosperms, most of which are evergreen and have aromatic, often red-tinged wood which in many cases is decay-resistant and insect-repellant. Several species have fine, durable wood used for timber and for cigar boxes, chests, and closets. The eastern red cedar of America is much used in cabinet-making, for posts, and in the manufacture of pencils.

Every home should have a cedar chest.

Made of genuine red cedar, mostly ornamented with 2-inch copper bands, studded with round copperhead nails, easy rolling casters, lined with satin, decorated with crucifix or plain cross. It hugs the body ever so comfortably. Clusters of pintucks add an elaborate touch. The clinging softness of real silk.

Lay up for yourself treasure in heaven, where neither moth nor rust doth corrupt.

Pirates' treasure trove.

Peach, white, flesh, Nile green.

THE USES OF ADVERSITY

JOEL OPPENHEIMER

the combination
of poisons
is called CHOP

this does not seem
to be an acronym
since in the names
of the four drugs used
only the letters c and p
appear as initials
although one of the drugs
has a common brand name
beginning with o

that still leaves
the letter h
to be accounted for

there is
cyclosphosphamide
plus doxorubicin
plus vincristine
which is the one
marketed as oncovin

these three
are pumped in
by injection

the fourth poison
is prednisone
i take this by mouth

the prednisone
leaves an acrid taste
that lingers
although that could
as well be caused
by the allopurinol
i take at the start
to offset the uric acid
produced in the body
by one of the other drugs

you can see this is
a complicated business
chasing malfunctioning
misfunctioning or
dysfunctioning cells
around my body
in attempt to stop
their choking growth

all three prefixes
mal mis and *dys*
mean the same thing
generally which is
bad badly wrong
wrongly ill or
difficult
          mal from
latin via french
mis from the teutonic
and *dys* from greek

all words break down
into their parts
even as you and i
even as you and i

❋   ❋   ❋   ❋

and so to
cyclosphosphamide

let me tell you
what i have found
about this poison
in the book the
government sent us

possible side effects
of this poison include

—and why *side* effects
when they are simply
effects said head-on

in any event
they may include
blood in the urine
and painful urination
either of which needs
immediate medical attention

as a consequence
it is important i drink
extra fluids so that
i will pass more urine

the next category is
side effects requiring not
immediate medical attention

but medical attention
as soon as possible

you see there are
fine distinctions
being drawn here
in my body

these effects include
black and tarry stools
cough
        dizziness
confusion
agitation
fever or chills
sore throat
side pain
stomach pain
joint pain

missed periods
only when applicable
and so not to me

shortness of breath
sores in mouth
sores on lips

what the doctor
referred to
using old language
as cankers
though i am sure
there is
a more precise
latinization
available to him
for obfuscation

but this is not
necessary
            canker
cancer chancre cancel
are all the same

shipley and partridge
agree
        the words come
from cancer the crab
and are originally
from *kar* meaning *hard*

and i find also
the news that *kar*
is the base for
all *ocracy* words
so once again
death and taxes
unavoidable

so
    sores in mouth
and lips
feet swelling
or lower legs
tiredness
unusual bleeding
or bruising

but what is usual
bruising or bleeding
i question
            no answer

unusual thirst
unusually fast heartbeat
unusually frequent urination

this is now the story
of my usual life
                    weakness
yes i have had that often

but not the last
of this list
yellow eyes and skin

i am also to check
with the doctor
if after receiving
this injection
i notice redness
or swelling or pain
at the site
of said injection

next are listed
side effects
needing attention
after i stop
using the medication

i am to check
immediately
if i notice blood
in my urine
is one such
as if going to pee
and peeing blood
would not prompt
some concern

listed last
are the effects
that usually
do not require
medical attention

darkening of skin
and fingernails
loss of appetite
unless severe
loss of hair
nausea and vomiting
again unless severe

so that turning
from a hairy
pot-bellied kike
into a bald
skinny nigger
is not to be
commented on

listen just writing
this list i develop
symptoms at
an alarming rate
one every thirty seconds
but i keep writing
and do not inform
my doctor
        why give him
the satisfaction

but keeping track
of all of them
and defining the words
severe unusual extreme
this is work enough

cyclosphosphamide
may be given
by either mouth
or injection

seven hundred
milligrams
come into me
by needle

❀   ❀   ❀   ❀

doxorubicin
on the other hand
is given only
intravenously

again i am
to drink
plenty of
extra fluids

doxorubicin
may cause urine
to turn reddish
in color

a red which may
stain my clothes
but this redness
is not blood
it says here

it says it is
perfectly normal
and lasts for only
one or two days

in fact my urine
showed such a
reddish tinge
ten minutes
after they put

the damned stuff
in me
        i hurried
from the cubicle
i'd sat in
for the injections
to the toilet
down the hall
before i saw
the doctor again
for further
instructions

everyone
            self
                    wife
nurse
        nurse's assistant
doctor
            all chuckled
at my quick response
to having some
eight hundred
milligrams what it
all adds up to
of fluid put in me

again i am to
watch for symptoms
requiring immediate
medical attention

irregular heartbeat
pain at the place
of injection
                    shortness
of breath
            hell

it's my damned lungs
at the seat of this
so of course i have
shortness of breath

swelling of feet
and lower legs
wheezing
              and if
doxorubicin
accidentally seeps
out of the vein
it may damage
some tissues
and cause scarring
so again i must
tell the doctor
or nurse right away
if i notice
redness or pain
or swelling at
the intravenous site

and again the list
of things needing
medical attention
as soon as possible
but not immediately

fever or chills
or sore throat
side or stomach pain
joint pain or skin rash
or itching
sores in mouth
or on lips
unusual bleeding
or bruising

if after i stop
using doxorubicin
i have an
irregular heartbeat
or shortness of breath
or swelling of feet
and lower legs
it would require
medical attention
but darkening of soles
or palms or nails
darkening or redness of skin
diarrhea unless severe
loss of hair
nausea or vomiting
unless severe
and reddish urine
are all normal
and usually
do not require
medical attention

eighty milligrams
of doxorubicin
go in me

✲   ✲   ✲   ✲

vincristine
is the third element
of CHOP
          i get
one milligram

vincristine
may require
special precautions

it frequently
causes constipation
and stomach cramps

again oh lord
the story of my life

my doctor may want me
to take a laxative
or a stool softener
but i am not to decide
to take such medicines
on my own without
first checking
with my doctor

again i am to drink
extra fluids
although with this drug
this may not
be necessary
so again i am to
check the the doctor

vincristine can also
damage tissues
and cause scarring
if it accidentally
seeps out of the vein
so again i am to
look out for
redness pain or
swelling at the site

there are new entries
in the list
of effects requiring
immediate attention

blurred or double vision
constipation
difficulty in walking
drooping eyelids
and i wonder how serious
that symptom can be
and if they are
kidding for once
or just checking
to see if i'm
paying attention

and the list goes on
headache
                    jaw pain
numbness or tingling
in fingers and toes
pain in testicles
again only
where applicable
in this case me
making up for
the non-applicable
missed periods
two medicines back

weakness
                    agitation
bed-wetting
                        confusion
dizziness or
lightheadedness
when getting up
from a lying or
sitting position
hallucinations

parenthetically
defined as seeing

hearing or feeling
things not there
so that everyone
is clear about
the meaning of
the multisyllabic word

lack of sweating
loss of appetite
mental depression
painful or difficult
urination
                seizures

doesn't this all
begin to sound
like being in love

don't we recall
sir philip sydney
and lord byron
both translating
catullus and catullus
himself i believe
culling from sappho

byron says it at length:

". . . though 'tis death to me,
I cannot choose but look on thee;
But at the sight my senses fly,
. . . trembling with a thousand fears,
Parch'd to the throat my tongue adheres,
My pulse beats quick, my breath heaves short,
My limbs deny their slight support;
Cold dews my pallid face o'erspread,
With deadly languor droops my head,
My ears with tingling echoes ring,
. . . life itself is on the wing,
My eyes refuse the cheering light,
Their orbs are veil'd in starless night;

Such pangs my nature sinks beneath,
And feels a temporary death."

and sidney in fewer words:

"My muse, what ails this ardour?
Mine eyes be dim, my limbs shake,
My voice is hoarse, my throat scorched
My tongue to this my roof cleaves
My fancy amazed, my thoughts dulled
My heart doth ache, my life faints
My soul begins to take leave."

claritas brevitas simplicimus
and sappho says
so mary barnard tells us
in even fewer words

> *pain penetrates*
> *me drop*
> *by drop*

so is it not love
these racing chemicals
and poisons chasing
down the cancers
chancres cankers
to cancel all
i ask you

and note here
that with vincristine
nervous system effects
may be more likely
to occur in
older patients
                 who i note
ought to be able
to distinguish
between these
and love

perhaps i am not
yet old enough for
such determinations

and once again i
may lose my hair

i keep thinking
of the woman
i saw in the
doctor's office four
years ago with
her mane of rich
black hair
              the doctor
saying if you're worried
she was bald
six months ago

hell no i'm
not worried
about my hair
beautiful
though it may be

perhaps it too
will grow back
full of youthful
vigor
        dark brown
and healthy
and not the
whited gray i
live with these days

and don't forget
my brothers
have been bald
since thirty

*   *   *   *

here we come to
the last element
in this witches brew

i take prednisone
not by vein
but by mouth
in tablet form
five each morning
each 20 milligrams
for ten mornings
and only after
a full breakfast

the pharmacist says
prednisone
is as near
to a miracle drug
as we can get
but one must be careful

well of course
miracles are not easy
things to handle ever

if i'm on prednisone
for a long time
i may need a low salt
and/or a potassium rich diet

stomach problems are
more likely to occur
if i drink alcohol
while taking this

in fact if i want
to take a drink

i must check
first with my doctor

of course i want
to take a drink

i've wanted to
take a drink since
that august day in 1970
i took the last one

which is a lie
but not deliberate
i swear it

clear as a bell
a warning bell
rang writing this
and i checked
the cough syrup
i take some nights
racked with coughing
keeping us awake
and it contains
1.4% alcohol
and i have not
checked that out

i will assume god
and the doctor
will allow me that

i must also
be careful before
having any kind
of surgery
including dental or
emergency treatment

to tell the surgeon
i am on prednisone

i presume that
removing my plates
in the evening
replacing them
each morning
is no emergency

if i were diabetic
this drug might affect
my blood sugar levels
and a change in
the results of
urine sugar tests
or any other
questions raised would
have to be checked

again there are
interesting additions
to the usual litany
tarry tarry stool sung
to the tune of that pop
hymn to van gogh's
starry starry night
and increased thirst
frequent urination
    in short
all the same old
fluidic questions

prednisone may also cause
skin rash acne
or other skin problems

whirling back now
to teenage love

or lack thereof

and mood or
mental changes
and muscle weakness
and seeing halos
around lights

oh poor van gogh
now they've got you
on this poison too

and the usual
stomach pain and
stomach burning

do they mean momma's
cooking that ring
of fire around my gut

unusual tiredness
or weakness
wounds that do not heal

for which i read
stigmata or
emotionally
as feuds

which leads to
wonder if those
who remain nameless
those mine enemies
also have these
these medicines
these cancers
growing in them

there is the

usual list of effects
needing attention
if they show up
after i stop
using prednisone

pain in abdomen
stomach or back
dizziness or fainting
fever and/or
continuing loss
of appetite
muscle or joint pain
nausea or vomiting
shortness of breath
unusual tiredness
or weakness
unusual weight loss

and then finally
those side effects
that usually need
no medical attention
unless prolonged or severe

indigestion
increase in appetite
nervousness or restlessness
trouble in sleeping
weight gain
false sense of well-being

what does it mean
if i feel okay

❀   ❀   ❀   ❀

CHOP is forced
into my body

to chase the
malefactors
cancers cells
chancres cankers
lesions tumors
call them as
you will
       they
have no place
in me and have
taken place here
and i will not
have them

i take CHOP
every three weeks
a time span
called a course

combining thus
the words *curse*
and *corse*: the body

BIRD IN AMBUSH

URSULE MOLINARO

The pretty-faced young woman lives on the groundfloor of an apartment hotel on Kaiulani Avenue, in the noisy heart of Waikiki. Except for the tropical vegetation intruding on her vision, she could almost be living in Times Square.

Where she hadn't lived when she'd been an art student in New York City. With money, & many friends. Only 3 years ago. When she'd lived in a loft in SoHo, on the 4th floor, above an art gallery that served Sunday brunches.

Kaiulani Avenue is named after the romantic young princess & heir to the throne, who allegedly died of a broken heart when Hawaii ceased to be a kingdom. The avenue used to be part of her park, where white peacocks wooed white peahens under enormous fragrant trees.

The pretty-faced young woman in the groundfloor apartment likes to think that some of the trees along her avenue date back to the princess's time. Like the enormous dark-leaved tree outside her window. It is covered with a constant snow of blossoms, which she can smell over the traffic fumes when she wakes up at 4 in the morning. & wonders if & when Princess Kaiulani smelled them, too.

If Princess Kaiulani wondered, as she wonders, if the fragrance span of flowers 2 hours a day for the large white orchid in her window box: from 10 a.m. to noon is a sexual advertisement, like the flashing of fireflies, the metallic treble of wooing birds. If Princess Kaiulani was curious that way. The way she is curious; or used to be.

The tree's fragrance seems to be strongest toward dawn. Although she's aware of perfumed wafts drifting into her window at other times of the night, when she lies awake, thinking about herself 3 years ago. Staring up at the full moon, waiting for it to dip behind the corner of the recent highrise further up the avenue. Where Kaiulani intersects with Cleghorn.

Sometimes she stands at her groundfloor window, naked in the full-moon light, & watches the couple of small gray-mottled island doves that recently built a nest in the lower saddle of the fragrant tree.

On stormy nights she can see their long-pronged feet clasped around a swaying branch, their huddled bodies rising & falling with the gusts. They look frightened, & she wonders if they are. If they don't trust their wings in wind. At night.

Sometimes she watches them in the afternoon, as they take turns on eggs she can't see from where she's standing, at her groundfloor window, naked in the sunshine. The brillo base or her pubic triangle flush with the window sill.

A little over 3 years ago, when she was living in her SoHo loft, she had shaved the letters Y I E L D into the thick red coils. To the applause of her friends who recognized her artword for the traffic signal she had intended.

Like the traffic signal at the intersection of Kaiulani & Cleghorn.

—the street is named for the Princess' British father, who must   YIELD   to enter the daughter's avenue.

Princess Kaiulani's parents were the opposite combination of the pretty-faced young woman's parents: her mother is British   or used to be   & her father is Hawaiian.

Which may be why her parents divorced: After a decade & a half of trying, a British wife & a Hawaiian husband may have dead-locked on who does what, in a household.

She can't tell if it's the male or the female dove that's sitting on the eggs, one white-fringed wing sticking straight up to air the wing pit.   —which she imagines crawling with lice.

She can tell the little doves' sex only when they're courting. When the male becomes a seesaw of self-abasement, dipping his head to the ground & raising his white-fringed tail, pursuing the scurrying female with metallic-sounding trebles he squeezes from his suddenly swollen pinkish throat.

She wonders how the females advertise their sexual readiness. If they advertise it. Perhaps it's all the male's idea, spontaneous yet ever-present, that makes him drop the piece of sandwich a tourist tossed, to pursue the closest female. Not too persistently. Ready to pursue the closest to the closest, if the first one scurries off too fast, too far.   —Prompted, perhaps, by memories of laying eggs.

The pretty-faced young woman watches the dove-feeding tourists, too, from her groundfloor window.

Honeymooners   of all ages; the Aloha shirts of the males matching the females' muumuus   who let go of each other's freshly ringed hand just long enough to break off a piece of bread. Who follow the doves' exaggerated courtship with tender smiles.

Recent parents, walking single file. Who collide as they stop to show the: pretty little birdies . . . to Buddha-babies in pouches strapped to their fronts &/or backs.

Couples in their thirties, with extended arms attached to children pulling to chase the scurrying little doves. Interrupting their courtship.

Frail-looking strays   unisex; of all ages   who carry crumpled bags filled with stale bread, or old rice. Who take turns leaning against another giant tree   a palm   on the sidewalk across the avenue, on specific afternoons. Feeding the gray-mottled little symbols of peace. From outstretched hands, in imitation poses of St. Francis. Or soaring national eagles.

They've become vaguely aware of her, watching. Vaguely aware of her nudity. Which makes them look furtive around the eyes, looking toward her window. & may or may not remind them of Amsterdam   naked women beckoning from windows overlooking canals if they traveled abroad before traveling to the islands. Where they may have settled; where the weather suits their frail-looking clothes.

The pretty-faced young woman wonders how long the little doves have been on the islands. If they were around when Hawaii was a kingdom, & escaped extinction because their feathers were considered too drab to be made into royal capes.

Perhaps they were brought to the islands by ships full of missionaries, & started breeding during Princess Kaiulani's time.   —Competing with the peacocks in her park.

She wonders if the Princess knew that the drab little doves are carriers of hepatitis. If they were carriers already then.

Perhaps they were, & the romantic young Princess had died of hepatitis   misdiagnosed as heartbreak   because she, too, had fed the little newcomers to her park. Letting them eat from her hands as she leaned against the same   then still skinny   palm trunk. The long white muslin sleeves of her dress flowing along her outstretched arms like wings.

If the pretty-faced young woman dies of hepatitis, it will not be from feeding the drab little doves.   —She only watches, from behind glass; & a wire screen.—   But from the cases of beer & bourbon   perhaps also from the dead chicken, an occasional coq au vin   her divorced parents take turns bringing her. In conscientious alternation, on specifically designated days of the week.

Her divorced father comes with bourbon & a dead chicken at 2 p.m. every Monday & Saturday. He spends most of the afternoon with her, drinking.

—& chatting. Which probably is harder on him than it is on her, squeezing metallic-sounding approximations of words past the mound of her tongue. She honks like a goose, or a tortured car horn.

It's a wonder her smile survived undamaged: 2 even rows of pretty white teeth.

Her divorced mother arrives breathless at noon on Tuesdays & Sundays. Drops 6 six-packs & a dead chicken/dead coq on her kitchen counter, pecks her on the cheek, & runs out again.

Tuesdays & Sundays are her divorced mother's bridge days, but her divorced mother agreed to tight-schedule herself rather than risk running into the father on bridgeless days.

Or into the therapist, who comes on equally bridgeless Wednesdays & Fridays.

Whom both parents conscientiously avoid, because of the way they both feel he looks at them, over his rimless glasses.

They also want to avoid walking in on her, standing naked at her window. Which has shocked both parents, on separate occasions.
    —It led to their setting up the rigorous visiting schedule; she now marks her calendar when to get dressed.—   Not because her parents are troubled by red memory flashes of Amsterdam, where they spent their honeymoon   —where she was conceivably conceived—   but because they interpret her lack of clothes as a lack of interest in her damaged body. In her continued handicapped life.

Which is also the interpretation of the therapist. Who also walked in on her standing naked at her window, one afternoon when he was early. When the Honolulu traffic had been unusually light.

The therapist was not amused but became furtive around his glassed-in eyes, like the stray-looking dove feeders across the avenue when she drew his attention to the dividing line of the window sill. How accurately the window sill divided her body into damaged & undamaged parts. Her unharmed top except for the contorted tongue   — her wayward left hip & foreshortened leg that make her look like a seesaw when she walks.
    He told her to get dressed while he went back outside to sit in his car. Then came back in to tell her about her lack of interest in the progress of her therapy.

She asked if he wanted a beer, or bourbon.
    Which unleashed a tirade about irresponsible parents. Who substituted alcohol for their much-needed presence. & weren't helping her at all to regain her speech. Or improve her walk. Which could be regained/improved only through patient daily exercise.
    . . . Instead of standing naked at the window.

She has asked him a thousand times: to lay off her parents. Who have nothing to do with what happened 3 years ago.
    Which happened because of gravity.
    Gravity defied by 4 tabs of LSD.

She is sitting on the blond wood floor in her SoHo loft. Surrounded by friends.

With glowing faces.

The walls are glowing.

The floor is glowing.

Outside her fourth-floor window the sky is glowing. Flecked with gold.

She stands up & stretches. She feels wonderful. She feels weightless. She tells her friends that she can fly.

They smile up at her. They nod: they know she can.

She stands in the open window, stretching her wings.

4 flights just wasn't enough: she honks at the wincing therapist. Giving him her prettiest smile. He furtively looks toward the window, as though to reassure himself that she lives on the ground-floor. When he knows that her hideous seesaw limp wouldn't prevent her from climbing 8   10   20   flights of stairs, if she wanted to. It only looks painful when she walks; she no longer hurts.

Besides, what   or who   would stop her from taking the elevator to the top of the recent highrise further up the avenue, where father Cleghorn intersects daughter Kaiulani.

Where the moon disappears on nights when it is full. When she lies   or stands   awake watching.

Listening to an angry female voice yelling from one of the lower lanais. Without letting up, like a hard tropical rain.

The voice sounds Caucasian. & projects gray-feather hair, & mottled skin. A pointed, beak-hard mouth that yells: Get away from me, you son of a bitch. Go away & stay away. Leave me alone!

There never is an answer.

The watching/listening pretty-faced young woman wonders how Princess Kaiulani would have felt about angry female voices protesting their winglessness to the fragrant night. Drowning the sleepy trebles of nesting little doves that have replaced the peacocks in her former park. Where her ghost hovers like a white muslin sigh above the still standing   still royal   palm.

THIS TIME

HENRY H. ROTH

I

Last time when he awoke in the sinister glossy green recovery room, he was hugged by a pretty, flat-chested nurse who nurtured him and whispered happily that he was all better. And she *was* proven correct.

This time, a fierce pain nailed him to the bed—the side slats barely contained his thrashing. Like an unwelcome jack-in-the-box, a stout grim nurse appeared. Later when his cries and quivering continued, she groaned impatiently, and politely insisted he try to be more still. Exhausted he looked away. Ok, ok, would he die soon or would this fanciful cancer attack, retreat, hit and run, and mug him for a dozen more rotting years? A tough-looking, overmuscled Spanish punk orderly joined the implacable fat nurse. He napped, awoke, cried out again, and lay quietly in his sweat. They finally noticed him; with dazzling grace, the orderly spun the bed out of the recovery room along the warped hallway floor into an open-mouthed elevator. Next they exited the massive elevator, and he, now safe not sound, returned to a room that was even smaller than remembered. Another luckless patient squirmed restlessly a few feet away. The nurse and orderly waltzed outside the room. He felt lost. The other wounded patient, sucking a hairy thumb, slept, desperately and loudly.

Each evening, a wife still thin, still pretty, and always punitive, visited his shabby quarters. She dutifully arrived after work and joined him for a miserable supper. Everything she wore, planned to the last detail, quickly became frayed and drab. *Fair*, not *fair*, he thought. Both had erred terribly; their life, heavy and dark, was a constant reproach. He acted out infrequently usually discreetly with drinking and occasional affairs. Delighted in telling splendid anecdotes. Loved the hurly-burly party and wanted a noisy, festive home. She could not deny or vanquish drink or sexual meandering, but avenging ruthless dictator, she punched air and life from his public stances and desires. He always ready to run to life, she licking her colorless lips, blotted it. Two sons sorted life out early, in time left for colleges in distant landscapes, and never returned. They did call every two weeks on Sundays, and their succinct letters and appropriate cards were not infrequent. He missed them greatly. She admitted nothing; they both hardened in an unfenced existence. She said he looked better. He insisted it wasn't true. Then both were silent. They ate carefully—lonely people no longer astonished by their loneliness. She told him the Chairman and the Dean of Humanities, among other colleagues, had called. He nodded, grinned, and pointed to droopy flowers and thick boxes of chocolate—visible gifts of how his pals worried about him and their own mortality. He knew they were all relieved that at the moment only immediate family could visit.

You do look better, she insisted. He grudgingly agreed with her, sure, ok, maybe I am getting better. She crumbled an odd-shaped chocolate-chip cookie. He wondered what she was doing here.

The newest nurse, a quicksilver erotic thing, offered superior drugs. The pain was shunted away to a distant ledge where it lurked for eight hours. He determined to dream of his newest nurse; instead there was another damn bus dream. He, a sole passenger in a ratty bus, traveling to vague lands, stopped at borders where diligent guards refused to let him continue. Always he awoke to a dream image of being abandoned, sitting cross-legged under a leafless tree.

However, this time the bus was not stopped as it sped past villages and cities with complete disdain for red lights, speed limits, and stop signs. When he awoke he spotted several doctors bent over his fallen roommate a few feet away. "Sorry, sorry," blurred voices whispered. "Why, why?" he shouted back. *"The man is dead."* For the first time since the operation his chest wound stopped itching. He only cared about himself. He spied the comrade he'd never spoken to being packed and zipped into a garment bag. And waved farewell.

II

Too soon, visitors were allowed, and like bad ideas they poured in. A careworn odd crowd of distracted colleagues—mustached, bearded, badly shaven, balding, paunchy, and smelling of the glory and rot of city life.

All of them, all of us, should be less careless in all matters, and be more confident in our easily acquired tenure. Look at me, he boasted, sure my replacement beguiles my classes with well-prepared fascinating lectures. Students now know me for a fraud! Enough, he warned, ruminating to excess leads only to masturbation. Enough! Nurses impressed by so many professors of all ranks treated him like a ruined rock hero. A largesse, he accepted humbly. Tired by all his duties as host to so many, he felt he might be able to sleep without a powerful pellet. He did not share this truth with his nurse. Greedily he gulped the sweet gift and washed it down with a bucket of water; ironies and cheap shots aside, he had been really glad to see his colleagues.

III

No solitary noise floated in from the outside and nothing doing in the silent absolute of the ward. No one mopped to a shrill fragmented tune, no soppy moans beckoned from the sleeping maimed, no static from the nurse's station, and no wrong numbers from anywhere in the world. After three in the morning and he still celebrated the splendid day; at first shuddering resentfully while his colleagues had thronged in as if he were some hit film the *Times* had ordered their readers to see immediately. But, soon it had erupted into a noisy shebang: though a party bereft of booze, food, or the most timid of love moves—it was a splendid occasion. Tossing in bed, he still reviewed happy snapshots that so stirred him, it was impossible to sleep. What a distracted petulant child he was fast becoming.

Afterward, she, still devoted wife of pain and anguish, had looked at him shrewdly and nervously as if he'd been caught stumbling in from boisterous times. And he'd foolishly spilled out recent anecdotes that displeased and rankled her; therefore, she ate her dinner sparingly, and left early. Then his sons, as if sensing her early exit, and the mood being lighter, both called, and all reassured each other how much they still cared for one another.

During the festive afternoon, he'd been accosted by Martin Cohen, a colleague of more than twenty-five years. The first of his peers to attain the fullest tenure, Martin despite his many years on earth was still not used to all six feet four of himself. Still clumsy in his moving parts, but the wisest of observers of the human condition, Martin Cohen elbowed his ailing comrade, and asked loudly, "Who's the lady in the paisley bathrobe walking so damn fast to nowhere?" He, for the past few days, gingerly tiptoeing around the premises, had wondered the same, had seen her walking well past the speed limit and for hours at a time. No mumbler or hallucinator, an intelligent look to all her good features, the obsessive walker was extraordinary, but clearly she was not loony. Cohen, impatient for answers, shook his large head, "She's a find, you lucky scoundrel. I like them slightly used up like me, like us. Mark my words, look her up." Then Cohen rambled about his newest grant proposal and bored the both of them. Almost four o'clock now, as he played back all the afternoon images, but only the woman's speedy hikes, around the floor around the clock, flooded his landscape.

IV

"Walk with you?" he asked a morning or two later. She nodded, bid him welcome, and didn't appear put off or surprised. She did not offer to shake hands when he introduced himself. Finally wise, he understood touching would come later.

They ambled along, conversing like old friends, catching up on recent news. And he had no trouble keeping up with her relentless pace.

His was cancer of the left lung; she had lost two breasts. Her gray eyes narrowed but did not tear when she said brightly, "I'm not forgetful, they're not misplaced boobs, you understand. They're gone." Unable to reply, though still the concerned suitor, he scanned the lady, and her body remained not uninteresting, indeed looked promising. She, as if sensing a careful scrutiny, posed but for an instant and then went off marching again. And her telling him, "It's doctor's orders to walk and keep walking, acquire a new balance to compensate my loss." He nodded sagely this time. "I was never full-breasted at all, but the body fiercely mourns all losses and punishes by making me stumble and forces my shoulders and back to sag." "No," he argued, "you're fine. You walk better than a queen." She bowed. He insisted, "We're both fine," and vainly attempted to keep pace with her jaunts. She turned to him, "My you were popular two days ago." "Proof of popularity," he defined, "is if the curious return." She laughed, "No one's curious about me at all." "Who've you told?" he wisely asked. She smiled thinly, "I've no wish to boast about dying." He looked away as if he might cry. She touched his shoulder. "Walk with me."

He only desired time alone with her. Gruff with any boorish visitors, he tolerated little small talk, insisting he required several naps in the afternoon. And his wife and he no longer ate together, and both were relieved. She, always eager to sleep alone, put out the garbage neatly and vainly tried to keep alive her shabby house plants. All the other times of day and night he and the woman roamed the wards and crannies of the hospital. The eight floors held no secrets and became their countryside.

Already they were nostalgic. How had they become friends so quickly? Both very shy, yet for once they lunged with boarding house reaches toward a center. And trust was immediate, confessions flowed like confetti and twirling banners. Nothing shocked or frightened them about each other. Both were obsessive, careful people, chewing over life happily and ruthlessly. And so they walked gossiping about the doctors, the nurses, their own concerns, their past and the present, but not daring yet to peek into the future. Once he said in delight, "We can have breakfast and lunch every day 'til Blue Cross interferes." She clucked, "And you have a patient wife in the wings for supper if you wish." And walked off, not teasing now. Angry too, he let her walk away, knew she must retrace her steps. When she returned he was at her side, like a puppy.

"Be forgiving," she apologized, "I'm ill."

He said, "I want to have supper with you."

"And walk with me," she asked.

Now they held hands and shocked a half-blind diabetic man who'd recently been shorn of a leg. Later that night the woman sing-songed to him, "Married twice, next I lived with a man who turned me out, when I was diagnosed. Though he sends flowers daily." "Bastard!" he cried out. Doctors, nurses, maintenance staff, volunteers, patients, guests pushed forward to get a better view.

"He needed nurturing though he was past fifty, and I can't give him these." She pointed angrily.

Other people moved in closer. He whispered, "You only need mending."

She, for the moment, looked too weary to walk. "We only need mending." Then she sped off. He followed slowly. The audience left quickly. He knew he'd catch up. He knew he'd catch up, or she'd slow down for him.

Another day he boasted, "My kids called again."

"They haven't visited?"

"I told you they live far away."

"So."

"So I told them not to come unless I was dying."

She said simply, "But you are dying."

He said, "They listened and stayed away."

"Did they always listen to you?"

"What good to see me convulse."

"Who then should be permitted to see you?"

"Only you," he said.

It was sunset. It was twilight. It was sunrise. There was a beach. A cove and a cottage. It was an asylum, a battered home, a hospital. Didn't matter whether it was a dream or not. All he knew was neither of them could sleep apart. Accidentally, they had to meet in the barren hallway—lonely trespassing people. It was such a quiet place now. A home with the rest of the family safe and sleeping. An outstanding image she confirmed, kissing him. They gently embraced. Both their aching empty chests were worse after the slight exchange. Then he asked her to his room. He gently yanked at her wrist; of course she followed.

Once inside the room, arching on the bed like hooked fish, they squirmed toward one another. Already his chest leaked, the set of her eyes revealed her discomfort, but moving slowly they almost discovered several ways to fold together. Finally at a sly angle he fastened to her, both agreed to a sweet cantering, and finally to the speedy gallop. Bruised, she spent the night with him; bruised too, he held her as close as he could; it was all done, promised, and decided on.

For hours she waited demurely for him in the visitor's lounge. When he finally arrived wan and shaken, his bathrobe a heavy curtain ringing his narrow body, she did not chastise him for thorough lateness since his room was a few feet from the lounge.

He sat gingerly next to her. "I couldn't bend all day," he apologized.

"Were you searching for something?"

"No why?"

"Why the need to bend?"

He held her carefully. "I want to be at my best with you."

She said, "Oh, it's too late for that, don't you see. And it doesn't matter at all."

She, adjusting her trim paisley robe, leaned to draw him up to her side; and giggling like teenagers they cruised noisily about the hospital.

This time, however, unlike rowdy unformed children, they were eager and able to accept their power and grace, and they were never the same again.

WORD BASKET WOMAN

GARY SNYDER

Years after surviving
the Warsaw uprising,
she wrote the poems of ordinary people
building barricades while being shot at,
small poems were all
that could hold so much
close to death   life
without making it false.

Robinson Jeffers, his tall cold view
quite true in a way, but why did he say it
as though he alone
stood above our delusions, he also
feared death, insignificance,
and was not quite up to the inhuman beauty
of parsnips or diapers, the deathless
nobility   at the core of all ordinary things

I dwell
in a house on the long west slope
of Sierra Nevada, two hundred mile
swell of granite,
bones of the Ancient Buddha,
miles back from the seacoast

on a line of fiery chakras
in the deep nerve web of the land,

Europe forgotten now, almost a dream—
but our writing
is sidewise and roman, and the language
a compote of old wars and tribes from some
place overseas. Here
at the rim of the world
where the panaka calls in the cha—the heart
words are Pomo, Miwok, Nisenan,
and the small poem word baskets
stretch to the heft of their burden.

I came this far to tell
of the grave of my great-
grandmother Harriet Callicotte
by itself on a low ridge in Kansas.
The sandstone tumbled,
her name almost eaten away,
where I found it in rain drenched grass
on my knees, closed my eyes
and swooped under the earth
to that loam dark, holding her emptiness
and placed one cool kiss
on the arch of her white
pubic bone.

WINGS

HARRIET ZINNES

He opened the door and saw the chair in the center of the little room. He was surprised of course. What visitor had displaced that chair, his Eames chair that never, simply never was moved from in front of his desk. He looked quickly around the room to see whether anything else had been moved. Had his apartment been broken into? He walked over to the desk itself, quickly glanced at his books and typewriter, then opened up the top drawer, shut that, opened the drawers on the side. Nothing touched. Nothing seemingly removed. He walked over to the large filing cabinet and again opened drawers. Again everything in place. He left what he called his study—a mere anteroom really—and walked into the living room. Had he raised the lid of his grand piano? He couldn't remember doing that. He looked at the couch, not at all disheveled, the chairs, the little tables, lamps in order. He again walked over to the piano. He was sure John had left his Schubert sonatas on the ledge of the piano. Wasn't he in the midst of rehearsing? And what was Satie's *Gnossienne* doing opened on the piano bench? He went into the dining room, glanced at the neat buffet, and then opened the drawers of the little chest in which he kept his mother's silver. Everything in place.

He then walked into his bedroom. Walked directly to his bureau to look at the drawers of his chest, especially the top drawer where he kept gold cufflinks, tie pins, and those silly gold chains that he never wore but that his first love, Ted Blight, had given him. As he

was opening the drawer, a strange voice called out to him: "Hi."
He turned abruptly, his heart pounding. What he saw was more a
little girl than a woman. A twelve-year-old girl (or was she a
woman?) was sitting propped up on pillows. His pillows! She kept
staring at him, smiling, holding him transfixed, as she casually took
out a cigarette lighter and lit a cigarette. "Smoke?" she asked.

"I never smoke in my bedroom—and don't allow anyone else to,"
he found himself saying sharply.

She smiled at that. "Rule Number One just broken."

Why didn't he retort to that or at least walk over to her, even run
over, and grab the cigarette from her mouth? He was certainly ca-
pable of doing a thing like that, especially under the anger he was
feeling. "I wish you'd put out that cigarette," he found himself say-
ing quietly.

"Oh, I'm not going to do that. I always smoke in bedrooms, espe-
cially the bedrooms of the men whom I have followed."

"Followed? You have been following me?" He was stunned. Had
he been so preoccupied lately about the play's possible closing that
he was not aware when he was being followed? "How long have
you been following me? And for God's sake why? Why have you
been following me?"

"One question at a time. I've been following you since I saw you
perform in *Oh! Calcutta,* and I've been following you because I like
you. This morning you happened to have left your apartment door
open—I gather you were late for your rehearsal—so that it was easy
enough for me to get in."

"Left my apartment door open? I am becoming absent-minded.
But how long have you been following me?"

"Three days. You see, it didn't take long to trap you."

"Trap me? Yes, that's it exactly. You have trapped me. Now that
you are here holding me entrapped, as it were, hm, now what do
you want of me? May I sit down at least?" Why on earth was he
asking her permission? She wasn't holding him at gun point. Merely
with her eyes, and that God-awful cigarette. "Will you leave now,
now that you have made your presence known and have found me
in my own apartment? Surely that is all you want. You may get off
the bed now, thank you."

"But that's exactly where I want to be. You are an idiot. Why do you suppose I've been following you if I didn't want to get into bed with you. Why?"

"You don't want to go to bed with me," he blurted out with astonishment. "Not with me. Don't you know, don't you know I don't like women!"

"I know," she said calmly, "but I like you, and there's no reason after all why you can't be trained to like me. I'm not that ugly, and at first I'll make very few demands on you. I've trained men like you before. You'll be all right. Don't worry. You may be my chief star. You may require only one lesson. Come here. Let's start our first session. It may be the last, really. Don't be shy. I won't hurt you."

He couldn't believe that he was walking toward the bed. What kind of witch was she? Not only did he walk over to the bed—the wrong side; he never slept on that side of the bed with his lovers—but he began to undress: took off his shoes, his socks, his jacket, shirt, tie, undershirt (that gorgeous pink one that Al so loved), and finally with just a little embarrassment his undershorts, pink bikinis, hot pink of course, with that daring scarlet-red border.

"You're doing fine," she said soothingly. "I'll start by giving you an encouraging kiss." Shivering, he accepted that light kiss. It was on his cheek, thank goodness, he thought. Why was he shivering, and why wasn't he running away? Why wasn't he throwing her forcibly off the bed?

"Look here," he found himself saying, "I don't want any more of your entrapment. I don't like women, and surely not little girls—are you twelve or thirteen, for heaven's sake—and this is my bed, my apartment, my life. Why why don't you get out of here, once and for all?" But his actions were belying his words. Imagine. He was kissing her on the lips, and he thought he heard all sorts of mad words as *darling dear sweetheart my love*. Whatever was happening here in his own bedroom? He wasn't chagrined or mortified. Maybe he was on the stage and just simply did not know where he was. He remembered his part in that Shaw play in which he was wooing that older woman. What was the name of the play? Wasn't he called Eugene or something like that? Maybe he was now on stage. "Are we rehearsing a play? Say, are we rehearsing a play? Tell me, what's my part like? Am I getting the leading role? Whom am I playing opposite? You're not my leading lady, are you? And what is your name? And how old are you anyway?"

At this point he recognized she had no energy for words. She was forcing him to enter her, and he was doing just that. Did the director call for the act itself? Oh God, wasn't he in a Broadway production? Was it just porn? Had he been shot into the twenty-first century where such things were permitted on the legitimate stage? What country was he in, what stage, what city, and above all what play—and did he have the leading role? But he suddenly felt himself spent, and threw himself off the little girl—surely she was just a little girl—and stretched out his arms across the bed. "You little witch," he said without any animosity, "you've tired me out: and I don't believe it, yes, you've given me pleasure. But what play are we in, what play?"

As he picked himself up and turned to her side of the bed, he was appalled that she wasn't there. Of course she's probably gone to the john. He waited for it seemed at least ten minutes. He hardly had the strength to get off the bed to look for her. At first he decided to call out. But what was her name? "Little girl," he began, "little girl, where are you? Are you in the john? Come out, will you? I've got to ask you more questions." No answer. "Little girl," he called again. "Where are you?" Still no answer. He'd just have to pick himself off the bed and investigate. Entirely nude (and he never let his lovers see him nude: it was his rule NEVER TO BE TOTALLY REVEALED) he walked toward the bathroom. The door was wide open. She was not there. He made a frantic tour of the apartment. She was no where to be seen. Should he try to run out to find her? Without his clothes? That would never do. No, he'd better run into his room and dress quickly for the pursuit. He was dashing into his room toppling his best marble table and adorable Tiffany lamp when the crash of the lamp called him to his senses. *But this is my opportunity to get rid of her. What am I doing trying to find her? Am I so bewitched that I can't even know when I have it good?* Trembling—still with the shock of his new delight and with the equally new discovery that he could get rid of a strange creature who had bewitched him, he sat down entirely naked on his favorite leather chair, snuggled up in it, and tried to recover his senses. The only action surely was inaction. He came quickly to that conclusion. His brain apparently had not been harmed. He could think straight and hard. That little witch had followed him and had had him. He had surely been had. And it was over. Relieved, he felt his back arch comfortably against the chair. He was just about to close his eyes with exhaustion and triumph, when he heard a small voice say, "Bye-bye my love. You were beautiful."

He looked up in time to see the little girl spread wings and fly directly out of his living room window. Luckily it's a French window, he thought. John was right when he chose that.

IOVIS OMNIA PLENA

ANNE WALDMAN

An excerpt

Mature love you say but my wounds come out through inner temple

which are participants containing a statue of . . . . . female
    personnel,

not subject matter, a tableau of outerspace, concubines?

where we had countless meals and struggles with any father.

What is the mature and conditioned space O Jove?

Dear Anne,

Please advise how I may develop a scintillating poetic pres-
ence. Last time I read most dozed off. I dislike Vergil. Result of
having to construe 40 lines a day at Choate—those endless similes

> As when at dawn the ducks
> from out the marsh
> Curdling their pintails in

the early starch
etc etc etc

Sorry, that's clammy armpit . . .

Very best to all,

JL

Never liked Jove either. Wd prefer to be inhabited

by Αφρωδιτη or some nifty Olympian girl.

It is a play or way to amuse the girl or is it? A way to talking

is another to journey to never abuse but wounds are fake and

are the scourge of me and they are real scourge of me. Where

to leave off talk of all these brothers and leave it here.

Dear Man Who Rends My Table And My Hearth: SCRAM!

I am a ruined table because
I met a maiden good
I walked into an explicit house
and was a trait of forefathers
They could arrest me in my cunning
But they are not the boss of me
They are not the actor in
a new phase of history: horse & chariot
They are not a grimace in this old gal's boot
We are like one city and another

And another comes along soon
the shape of Neptune's face
or Saigon, a sight for the broken
heart of anything
It is the ancient place of Ur
It is your own place won in fair fight
giving the lie to property tax
and the language of my people
O Male Civilizations!
I am not a party to my gold
but relate what has gone past
once the sufferings are over
Are they ever? I doubt it
But they are done to a crisp
and die in cold light
I am a regular next winter
I am a vestal in my propensity for service
I stretch my neck with music
but I doubt the way The Prophet
goes about bringing them to the Mount
Not doubt but a kind of wonder
It is a fiery night
and proud Maisie stalks the wood
She is the maiden of me
She is the good of me
I am a time table for anything wet,
for anything with star and waxing moon
I am the dream of me, mere
illusory scales & fins, webbed toes
I grow into the scout of me
the densest one who reports back
to the head of me and sprouts
the garden you put your mind to
one sunny day
It glows like pregnant thing
and grows the seed of any Art
It is alive nor is
the heart of me dead
I go so that a windless bower be built

So that I go quietly, I go alone
I am alone and delight in how speech
may save a woman
How speech is spark of intrusion

Letter to Miss Idona Hand

Washington July 15, 1903

My Dear

I suppose you rec'd a postal from me by Tuesday noon—I thought you would be anxious to know weather we arrived safely or not. We have had a splendid time. I cannot describe the beautiful sights we have seen it is something wonderful. I and the boys are sitting in the Pennsylvania depot. They are waiting while I write this small message. We just saw the house where Garfield was shot. We have covered a good bit of ground since arriving but we have several places yet to visit. I am trying to make a note of everything so I can explain it to you. But next summer you must see things for yourself. This is the most beautiful place I ever saw. Everybody is feeling well we have a few jokes on one another. When we first arrived we walked down Sixth Street and we wanted 452. Charlie looked and saw the number 859 and called it out. It was a sign saying established 1859. You want to ask him if he stopped on Establishment Street. This morning I awoke about 6 o'clock their was a bell ringing it rang twice and then commenced ringing harder. I said Boys their is a fire. I lit out of bed in a hurry. They are having fun about that. Well Dear I must close now hoping this will do you some little good. I will be home about Saturday and tell you all about it.

yours

John

What are you you are what are you are you what seems lady?

Idona's seamed stockings in the attic, John a Protestant

never protesting on the porch, a gentle man outside any

war, born in the gap between worlds in collision.

All the lovers getting out of the army for one sane reason

or another, generation skipped. The grandfather in white,

father in Khaki I won't skip over them to what you are

You're a pistol eye a mistletoe a missile man a Marxist

You're a sword eye a job queen a devil-may-care

You're a conch a knob you guys are slobs

We're playing tick-tack-toe you're a sticky glue-stick

but a stick-in-the-mud too are you

You're spaghetti-hair Dad, you crazy old man

You woman Daddy you New York Times reader

You New York Times reporter

You're a suitcase   What? What are you?

You're east of the sun & west of the moon

Are you are you are you are you   What? What are you?

You slob you rubber band nose

You're a bully and a mean-shoot a paper clip a peppercorn

You've stuck in my teeth

You're a European walrus

You're a blue muscle you're a red tomato

You crossbow you arrowhead you man-of-me

You're a bellow of church

You're a bump thump bump dummy

You're a broken down hospital

you're a cracked people

You're craggy rock cliff

You're Michael Jackson you're Jacky Frosty

You cup nothing

You're a hundred thousand bristle blocks

you're a peony—means you're a broken down housebell

You are my wife Mommy you are the dream of me

> The keep & key of an unruly person
> absorbed everyone & you realize he's
> only wild since noon

you're just out there looking at the moon

> So great my love on my male partners
> I have to leave town

(When you look into it on any person's desk
The town appears small)

so now

I RISE BEFORE ISHTAR IN THE EAST
I RISE BEFORE ISHTAR IN THE EAST

Moon disappearing
all's sluggish, dull
What's the color
Pronounce it windless
A shroud song is sad
sword cuts   who?
Some wicker man staggers
Listen to the Peregrine fall
I try, towered upon a short stretch
Seeing Mother meshed with herself
O dire is her Mother need
She's shortened loose
She's in the fittings
Windows iced into dark holes
are quiet
But I think of a dream
in green jasper
It goes like this:
something shattered in chips
sailing down   (was it?)
long cannels
cut channels
Something like Hawaii
for the craft
Need sharp eyes here
for a pagan sea

Lights stand up
in a dark wood
I'm now swimming in night green
"I shall paint my body red & dance"
she said I
will wear antlers or a
bone blooded with Earth-Time

I will
I will

In sets, sets in with her
holding tight slips
Those Martian canals are
cracked ice

I cut to the Andromeda movie
"Venus" is here too
I thought my body green or faun
& dropped the sexual stick
Shadows showed the crater
to be a New Moon
A storybook pomegranate split
She's got a myrtle whip
She made her name in whips
& made me worship her
Me, a mere shadow of sight
standing in the shell of the dream
eyed back into dark ovals
Of all the Pagans I was One
What oath is mine?
Who wouldn't bend to a
Virgin standing on the moon?
Can't resist
I'll paint myself white
You paint yourself red
We'll dance to a
Low Eastern Bright Eye tune
& follow that song
Our bedsheets will be like fire & ice
& I'll have to walk out
the next door
to close out the smell of you
                              (with BR)

THE CREATIVE IS SPEAKING It is a large you-name-it-machine
        made

of words to show you O Princes what's the side of He-Who-Risks

all for me, he the Bull leaper for in Bulls does the Earth-shaker

delight for in bulls does she know her truth & set down this

soft earth bed too grosse for Heaven upon which I end where

I begunne. (His loin cloth will be immaculate and bright,

his bracelets will be costly, his hair curled, his face painted

red & black for a night of love)

THE CREATIVE IS SPEAKING to write a nuclear warhead, to

walk inside itself circumscribed as an obtrusive lope. The

man wants to play the music loud to think he's some kinda animal

some kinda some kind some kinda animal

Douse him or send him into the next votary's mind

He's some kind some kinda animal

Not that he's untameable but ancient you know like a

tryseerotops which is not to say it died by living

out its need

& needed more than one of us

Touched him she thought he thought
Some space between

He said about sex all over again

She said Here I go again

A couple mentions the "you" factor

you know then

She's ready too

We hold out our hearts

So what's the suffering all about?

THE CHEATIVE IS SPEAKING How the sons of immigrants go
    back

to fight in the ancestral homelands. Now you know you are
    American.

Now you know how this is preserved in memory

You know how memory is cunning

That sex is early on the girl's mind

Now you know all manner of speaking openly

The myths are alive for a time

I come out full grown out of my father's split head

and am armed for the battle of love

These words are in answer to an assignment to make sense of
3 and 5

I represented my mother back to Greece

Poo EEE Nay EEE stah sohn ton lay o for EEE on?

There is not more hope than this: to find the right bus
Athens, which is a city built on the extension of Hestia's hearth
The head split in two and something is noticed in the duality
of city life: in and out, the inner and outer working daily
for the virgin spinster who would like to make sense of all
these trade routes, know who went where when and the little
amphora handles are clues to great travelers with goods who
plunged ahead to carry with them their genetic structures
among other things, & all the manifestations of all the
senses: color, texture, taste, smell, sight

The spice of night

The silk of midday

The clear soup of morning

A way of studying stars

A photograph of a king

The queen's proclivities

The way people might decide on a crime & so on

On returning from Egypt I had

1 hookah

2 scarves of silk, red as my fantasy of the red in Red Sea

& 1 Mediterranean blue

1 scarab pin (imitation)

Another scarab was lost in England in the room of the lady

who said "Scarabs always get lost around me"

And from these places I brought a new appetite for a

particular olive

It was the olive branch and owl which symbolized the way men lived before they were civilized and somewhere out of darkness I went to meet them.

Dear Lady,

I am an ingenious amature inventor. For five years I meditated on trying to produce as many new good invention ideas as I could. I did think up about 50 of them. After checking patentability I discarded 12 of them and had 38 left. When I tried to sell some to a few businessmen, I got two of them stolen. I got them witness and disclosure documents on the rest. I then sold one to a lady and then am now offering any or all the 35 inventions for sale to you now. I trust you enough to take a chance anyway. Many of these are cheap and easy to build and make. All have good money making profit potential, some many millions profit potentially. I am not at this time financially able to afford getting any patents because I am getting by just barely. I hope to sell 10 or 12 of my new Inventions and then patent two or three then myself. I did get your name from the Who's Who book in America and address. Rest easy though I'm only sending a few letters to a few ladies to try my luck and will not advertise my invention or write to any men at all about any inventions. Read the next page for more details and bless you regardless of your decision.

from Kenneth Alexander Walker

Brief Indication List of Invention Ideas of Kenneth Alexander Walker

1. Device for air improvement in homes.
2. New type of pet bird cage. Should be liked by bird lovers.
3. New type of child's tricycle.
4. New type of ladies watch band.
5. New type of styleish sun protection for eyes.
6. New type of loud noise control hearingwise.

7. New type of eyeglass frames. Should make people feel better.
8. New type of outdoor bird house. Bird lovers should like this one.
9. New type of barometer.
10. Improvement for safer night driving.
11. Burgler catcher mechanism.
12. New type of life raft.
13. Improvement for all replacement car door lock knob.
14. Method of getting massage while driving vehicle.
15. New type of food freezer. Should keep food frozen quality longer.
16. New type of refrigerator. Should keep food fresher longer.
17. New type of fish aquarium. Pet fish lovers should like.
18. New type of small animal cage for pets pet animal lovers should like.
19. New improvement for pet bird water dishes.
20. Method of improvement for men's briefcases.
21. Improvement on photo grey sun protection.
22. A camera and film picture improvement.
23. Improvement for teachers' blackboard pointers.
24. Improvement for telephone handles.
25. New type of scalp massager.
26. New type of wax candle. More light for its size compared to others.
27. Improved clothing iron women will like.
28. Light increasing lampshade electricity saver.
29. Directional light increased electricity saver.
30. Shark repelling life jacket.
31. New type of stove that is an improvement.
32. Flexible light aimer improvement.
33. Auto window washer improvement.
34. Drinking water cooler improvement.
35. TV commercial alternative improvement.

To His Excellency Mobutu Sese Seko
   Head of State

Citoyen President:

I appeal to you for the immediate and unconditional release of Tshisekedi wa Mulumba, a lawyer and former member of the Zairian Assembly who was arrested last October.

I believe that Mr. wa Mulumba is a prisoner of conscience, held solely for his non-violent exercise of fundamental human rights. He is reportedly held at Makala Prison in Kinshasa.

Thank you.

Anne Who-Grasps-The-Broom-Tightly

IOVIS OMNIA PLENA The world is full is full of you my lingering one, lingam of any century of this old papa's realm of this sweet fuck & sweat. Dear Father who made me so to be a poet on the battlefield of Mars, whose seed got dipped, got used & cannibalized to be this witness such and eke out her income her life her light on a bed of love, earth is my is my number O earth is the number to be joined by you old grandfather sky and harking back to he who is the genetics to any plump German girl, or any paranoid Huguenot daughter. I can take him or leave him, juiced out over many wars:

                                        & all these messages
                                            are the light
                                                of me
                                                      the life

                                                of me who receives them in the guise
of anyway you want

                                hemmed in . . . .
                                lost
                                willful
                                prepubescent in the long lunchroom hour . . .
                                I conquer you

A personal message:

Dearest Anne, there is so much more I wish I could say to you. This test has been enjoyable and frustrating in equal amounts. Sometimes I wonder why I bother, but when I hear you and certain colleagues of yours read, it at times seems worthwhile.

Looking at you, I see a romantic, an idealist, and a revolutionary. You seem to call it the way you see it, and have no qualms about nailing the "jello faced abominations" (My line) to the wall. You don't have any aversion to graphically describing sexuality, pain, life, death, the reality of what it means to be men and women.

If I seem nihilistic and cynical, it is because I am a heartbroken utopian dreamer and romantic who has slammed up against the grey wall of reality a considerable number of times. I live for vengeance, a sort of "poetic justice."

I admire how you with your greater experience of years and life than my own can still see so much "basic goodness." But you are still willing to call a cat a cat, a dog a dog, a man a man, and a woman a woman. And blame few indeed for what they inherently are.

I really would like to be a successful novelist, and my audience response at this most recent reading was better than usual, and I got positive feedback from Rick Andy Tom. Poetry is even more fun than drugs, you were right about that.

I got Bill Burroughs (Sr.) up on my wall smoking a joint and looking right through you. There is beer in the fridge, Joan Armatrading on the radio. Whatever you would tell me, I probably would take it serously.

The battle with the "Ugly spirit" is not to be discounted. Me and my whole little faction of friends and lovers wave at you, smile, flip the bird, blow a kiss from '77 '81 '83 '84. Here in exile I wish to know how I can best serve all those I left behind.

Gregory Corso said something to the effect of "If you take your shit and show it to some guy and he say THIS SUCKS you gotta say, fuck you man, your full of shit I'M A POET."

Burroughs said "There will be no self pity in the ranks."

I would really like to have THE DEFINITIVE QUOTE from

you. And if you want to tell me I have the whole damn thing
wrong, I'll listen.

Fer-ever yours, your hopelessly sentimental and incompetent
warrior in disgrace—

DM

D'accord that is the place to be, d'accord with him a place

to go down down on him with no music to prop this boy love

I extend to boy

It is the truth of me when I needed him and I was hard on him

& he in me, hard in me

to stay to prop this boy love

to be this fast hard boy love in me

I be it

in me, in me

to fast this love to fasten as I was hard on him to prop

his love

a violation & a forgetting   to prop all love

for I was hard on him to be a boy & love of the boy to be

a boy

go by, boy

yours in the ranks of any promise of manhood

& you are no music

you are no manhood yet

you are wonder I am spectator once   O boy!

Ye Guelfs, listen! This makes sense . . .

INITIATIONS

KIRK ROBERTSON

HOW TO JOIN THE LITTLE FIRE FRATERNITY

plunge your arm
up to the elbow
in hot coals
light corn husks
eat them

be able to see
into your body
& let Cougar
Bear Badger or Wolf
live there

be torn limb from limb
your arms & legs
thrown into the fire

& rise in one piece
in perfect condition

take the hearts
from butterflies & dragonflies

mix them with roots & blossoms
drink the sun then

sit around & bullshit

HOW TO JOIN THE ANT FRATERNITY

go over
the southern road
to Red-Ant's hills

step firmly
on a deserted hill
& extend your right foot
over the hill
then stand on your toes
stoop over the hill
& pray

use a broom
brush from the sick naked body
showers of pebbles
shot into it
by ants
who've been brought
to the surface pissed off

at being pissed & stepped
on

HOW TO JOIN THE RATTLESNAKE FRATERNITY

accidentally

step on a bowl of medicine

in front of the altar
break it
spilling the medicine

turn over a carving
of Rattlesnake
into the spilled medicine

bathe it

HOW TO JOIN THE SPIRAL SHELL FRATERNITY

sprinkle piss
on a heated stone
crush medicine over it

don't fail
to undo the knots
by rolling it in your hands
until it drops
in four pieces
at your feet

stay in your house
four weeks
before wearing your mask
or it will stick
to your skin
break it
drive you crazy
you'll die in four days

have your nose pierced
& an eagle plume inserted
while the blood is lapped
from the wound
by your brothers

don't fuck for a year afterwards

then capture Wood Rat
roast him eat him
so that your blood might be pure
when you start

fucking
again

HOW TO JOIN THE EAGLE DOWN FRATERNITY

paint your feet & legs
to the knees
& your hands & arms
to the elbows
white

don't eat
animal food or grease

cure the sick
by dancing

HOW TO JOIN THE FRATERNITY THAT DOES NOT FAST FROM ANIMAL FOOD

never eat jackrabbit
instead be able to hold

a hot coal

in your mouth

HOW TO JOIN THE HUNTERS FRATERNITY

play with live coals
rub them on your body

kill your prey by smothering it

then wash its blood
from your hands
over the fire

with water from your mouth

HOW TO JOIN THE CACTUS FRATERNITY

be male

kill an enemy
but don't take the scalp

be cured of a wound
arrow bullet or dog bite

be struck by flying cactus
at an outdoor ceremony

don't fuck for five days
after joining

or cactus needles
will fill your flesh

HOW TO JOIN THE GALAXY FRATERNITY

have medicine so strong
that if taken alone
your intestines would burn

be able to eat shit
drink piss

decorate yourself with mud
from the spring
travel with laughter

eat the most
bits of old blankets
splinters of wood

bite the heads from living mice
chew them tear dogs
limb from limb
fight over the liver

eat the intestines

HOW TO JOIN THE SWORD SWALLOWERS FRATERNITY

don't eat sweets beans squash
peaches or coffee
only game

don't fuck for four days

be able to freeze the corn
if you danced
in summer

be able to swallow a sword
from middlefinger tip to elbow
in length while dancing

then drink whisky & watch

for the morning star

HOW TO JOIN THE STRUCK
BY LIGIITNINC FRATERNITY

survive.

WATER MUSIC

JOHN FREDERICK NIMS

Ἄριστον μὲν ὕδωρ . . .

"Nothing noble as water, no,
    and there's gold with its glamor . . ."
Pindar on trumpet—First
    feisty Olympian Ode to the horseman,
Daring us, across the years:
Look to excellence only.
Water, you're pure wonder! here's
February, and on the pane your
    frost in grisaille shows how you flowered
    all last summer; it
Stencils clover, witchgrass, mullein
    meadow; between boskage gleam
Shores of Lake Michigan, her snow pagoda, junks of ice.
Farther off, spray and breaker, and your clouds
That hush color to a shadow as they pass,
While snowflakes—just a few—go moseying

Around . . . over . . . That cloud-coulisse
    valentine of a window!
Back of its ferny scrim
    scene after scene of a gala performance!
"Water's Metamorphosis,"

That's the show, and in lights too,
Booking all the world for stage.
Now let's make believe there's a magic
  camera, sensitive only to
  water molecules,
Loading film that blueprints hidden
  wetness in things—profile bold
But pearly the pulp of it: highrise, traffic, elm, marquee
Like electronic pointilliste machines;
On sidewalks, prismatic people, prismy dogs;
Ice-palaces for home. They effervesce

     Of course. Water's alive with light.
       Spawned of the ocean, life's macromolecules
     Begot history and time;
       culture their afterthought. Our own
     Body: mainly bog. Like
       trees walking? No. Walking waves
     Are what *we* are. Flesh briny. Our bone-shack sways
       to, smells of, the sea wrack.
     If we're stormy, halcyon too,
       no surprise, with such
     Surf, doldrum, and seiche in us.
       Alcoholic? Some.
     Water-freaks? Every last one. (All but death,
     Old bonehead who, teetotaling, totals all.)
       Thanks to wet ways, we live here.

You've seen films of the Hindenburg?
  Sky afire and the human
Rain from the clouds? But that's
  hydrogen's way: a psychotic companion
Turning—in a flash—berserk.
As for oxygen: sulphur's
Cousin, arsonist, a false
Friend to metal, apt to explode our
  sleepy haze of sawdust or wheat.
  Sickrooms venture its
Name in whispers. Breathe it straight a

while, and your throat burns, your head's
Logy, disoriented—you're a weakfish gulping sky.
(Nitrogen-thinned, it's breathable.) We've two
Irate djinns here—and what kabbalahs compel
Their spirits to that peace in H_2O?

Strange, that water's a blend of fire
   when it's flame that she hates and
Hisses, her molecules
   angled like arrowheads tooled for a crossbow,
Blunt, just 104 degrees.
Agincourts in the faucet?
Why not? Hi-tech myths can ape
Many an apeman supersitition.
   Yet if not twined lovingly—these
   two explosives—my
Wineglass here could turn *grenade*. As
   water reminds us, the world's
A maelstrom of lava beneath her easy circumstance.
All matter's smoldering at the core. Old-
Time Jehovahs—brimstone and the flood on tap—
Might better have let hydrogen relax

      Its double bond to oxygen—
         which would have shown the folk, given folk to show
      Just who *was* Who, as most
         things evanesced to zero space
      —Most, including people
         Water's our friend. Faucet-flow
      Around finger endears, the way kittens do.
         It blandishes bourbon
      As it mellows (fluid and cube)
         fire to amber, with
      Glass melodies. Diamond, ice
         crystallize alike
      (To the eye); ice though is good-humored, and
      Come spring, will restore playhouse and beach to us,
         melt to mellifluous tilth.

Besides, diamond's a liar—*poof*
   and it's soot when the heat's on.
Calling their glaciers back,
   Ice Ages warmed to us, left the lea greener.
What would Diamond Ages do?
Shrink-wrap countries in rock-glass,
Leave the planet strangled, sky's
Lavaliere, a Tiffany bijou
   glinting frigid fire. And would you,
   Diamond-Age young girls,
Cherish dewdrops, think them jewels to
   pretty your hair with—eyes brave
Through the damp of your lash before the livid avalanche?
Let's be glad—most of us anyway—we're
More dew-sort than diamond-kind. And there's the myth:
What suckled Aphrodite, sea or stone?

Festooned Sicily shore?—where foam,
   all glissando and swell, wreathes
Buoyant the swimmer. Dream:
   eastward in Eden once sparkled a garden
More delicious even than
Sappho's: apples blew perfume
Through liana languors; brooks
Wove their watery spell; mid-grove a
   Presence walked in cool of the day.
   No one dewier
Than that human pair, pellucid
   two, in the sun-flickered shade
By the pools, on a ferny tussock banked like pouffes. No one
Dewier? *You* were! that rickety pier
Once! your shoulders bubbling moonlight as you swam
And then—spirit of water, lithe—gleamed bare

     As moon on the pier, hair swirled back,
       laughing at me, "Last one in . . . !" Prismatic girl
     (Like those glorified trans-
       lunar dancers that Dante saw)

Sprinkled me with chill lake's
   mischievous fire. Now the tears
Are like fire to think . . . think . . . what I've thought and
      thought.
   But safer to think small:
Summer thunder, hail on the lawn;
   cuddling scotch-and-hail,
We blessed it as "heaven-sent!"
   Mostly water is.
Pray that it keep us. Our blue globe in space.
Our grand loves. Our least ones—like this spindly rose
   rambling on Pindar's lattice.

EDITORS' NOTE

Among the "Eight Poems" of Delmore Schwartz's later years included in *New Directions* 51 (1987) was "I Rejoice That Things Are As They Are." Upon closer reading, we discovered that the poem is in fact a transcription, with slight variations, of lines 20–33 of Section I of T. S. Eliot's "Ash Wednesday." We regret our error and reprint below the text in its established form.

I rejoice that things are as they are and
I renounce the blessèd face
And renounce the voice
Because I cannot hope to turn again
Consequently I rejoice, having to construct something
Upon which to rejoice
And pray to God to have mercy upon us
And I pray that I may forget
These matters that with myself I too much discuss
Too much explain
Because I do not hope to turn again
Let these words answer
For what is done, not to be done again
May the judgement not be too heavy upon us

NOTES ON CONTRIBUTORS

DAVID ANTIN has published ten books of poetry since 1967 and has been doing "talk poems"—speculative and narrative improvisations—since 1971. His two most recent books of talk poems, *Talking at the Boundaries* (1976) and *Tuning* (1984), are published by New Directions. A large selection from his earlier work, *Selected Poems 1963–73*, will be published this fall by Sun & Moon Press.

CAROL JANE BANGS manages programs in literature at The Centrum Foundation in Port Townsend. Her poems have most recently appeared in *Ploughshares* and *The Seattle Review*. New Directions brought out her 1984 collection, *The Bones of the Earth*. "Existentialists" is her first published story.

Born in Tasmania in 1940, CARMEL BIRD lived and studied in France, Spain, and California before settling in Melbourne. Her first American publication, *Woodpecker Point & Other Stories*, is forthcoming from New Directions.

Poetry editor of the British literary magazine *Ambit*, EDWIN BROCK has published six books with New Directions. His work has appeared in such American magazines as *The New Yorker, Antaeus*, and *The Partisan Review*. He is currently at work on a new collection.

FREDERICK BUSCH lives in upstate New York, where he teaches English at Colgate University. Some of his recent books include *Sometimes I Live in the Country, Too Late American Boyhood Blues*, and *The Mutual Friend*, all available from David R. Godine, Publisher.

Born in Schwerte, West Germany, in 1942, RÜDIGER KREMER studied at the universities of Münster and Bremen and from 1968 to 1972 was an editor at Radio Bremen. Now a free-lance writer in that city, he has completed a trilogy of poetry volumes: *Donald-Donald* (1980), *Lauter Gefilmte Personen* ("Just People in Films") (1983), and *Die Katzen des Königs der Spatzen* ("The Cats of the King of Sparrows") (1985). BREON MITCHELL, whose translations of Kremer's work have also appeared in *ND27, ND33, ND41,* and *ND43,* is the recent winner of the American Translators Association Prize for German Literary Translation for *Heartstop* by Martin Grzimek (New Directions, 1984). He is now at work on a volume of Siegfried Lenz's selected stories.

A former newspaperman and U.S. government official, ERNEST KROLL has published five volumes of poetry, and his work has been reprinted on paper, vinyl, and even granite. The last refers to two lines from his poem, "Washington, D.C.," which have been cut into the floor of the new Western Plaza on Pennsylvania Avenue.

A new collection of MICHAEL MCCLURE's poetry is expected soon from New Directions, publisher of many of his books, poetry (*Antechamber and Other Poems, Fragments of Perseus, Jaguar Skies, September Blackberries, Selected Poems*) as well as plays (*Gorf* and *Josephine: The Mouse Singer*).

URSULE MOLINARO, the author of *Nightschool for Saints* (Archer Editions), *Positions with White Roses* (McPherson), *Remnants of an Unknown Woman, The Original Trash Novel* (Red Dust), lives in New York City. Her work also appeared in *ND43* and *ND46.*

Editor of the literary magazine *Conjunctions,* BRADFORD MORROW has recently published his first novel, *Come Sunday* (Weidenfeld & Nicholson).

Former editor of *Poetry* magazine, JOHN FREDERICK NIMS has published volumes of poetry (among them *The Kiss: A Jambalaya,* Houghton Mifflin, 1982 and *Selected Poems,* University of Chicago Press, 1982), essays (*A Local Habitation,* University Michigan Press, 1985), and translations (*Sappho to Valéry: Poems in Translation,* Princeton University Press, 1980).

JOEL OPPENHEIMER lives in Henniker, New Hampshire. His recent books include *Why Not* (White Pine, 1987), *New Space: Poems 1975–1983* (Black Sparrow, 1985), *Poetry: The Ecology of the Soul* (White Pine, 1983), *At Fifty* (St. Andrews, 1982) and *Just Friends: Friends & Lovers, Poems 1959–1962* (Jargon Society, 1980).

Born in Marseilles in 1937, JEAN ORIZET spent his early youth in the Midi. By 1962, when he first published his poetry, he had studied Latin and Greek, simultaneous translation (English/Spanish), and diplomacy. Since then he has published twelve volumes of poetry, won the Prix Apollinaire (1982), and traveled widely, giving readings and lectures. Among ALETHA REED DE-WEES' translations are plays by Charlotte Delbo (staged at the University of Texas at Dallas) and René de Obaldia (staged at Southern Methodist University).

Forthcoming from New Directions is ISTVÁN ÖRKÉNY'S (1912–1979) *More One-minute Stories & Other Writings.* In 1982 New Directions introduced the Hungarian author to an English-speaking audience with his two novellas, *The Flower Show/The Toth Family.* JUDITH SOLLOSY'S family left Hungary when she was a child, and she grew up and was educated in the United States. After her marriage to a Hungarian filmmaker, she moved to Budapest, where she now works for the publishing firm Corvina.

British poet PETER READING was born in Liverpool in 1946 and attended the Liverpool College of Art, where he trained as a painter. Secker & Warburg has published many volumes of his poetry. He received a Cholmondely Award for Poetry in 1978 and the first Dylan Thomas Award in 1983.

ANTHONY ROBBINS's poems are from his manuscript *Not the Poised Moon.* Other poems of his have appeared (or will appear shortly) in *American Poetry Review, Partisan Review, Southern Review,*

New Letters, Sulfur, Exquisite Corpse, Yellow Silk, and *Pulpsmith.* He lives in Baton Rouge, Louisiana.

Driving to Vegas, KIRK ROBERTSON's collection of new and selected poems from 1969 to 1987, will soon appear from Sun/Gemini Press. It will be his seventeenth poetry collection. He is editor/publisher of Duck Down Press and lives in Fallon, Nevada, and is currently Director of Programs for the Nevada State Council on the Arts.

Rutgers University Press will publish HENRY H. ROTH's novel, *The Cruz Chronicle,* in the spring of 1989, and a collection of stories the following spring. A professor of English at the City College of the City University of New York, he has published more than a hundred stories. "This Time" is part of an ongoing series about urban university life entitled *Notes of an Adjunct.*

JEROME ROTHENBERG's seventh book with New Directions, *Khurban & Other Poems,* will be published in 1989. His most recent title is his *New Selected Poems 1970–1985,* a companion volume to *Poems for the Game of Silence, 1960–1970.*

Translator, essayist, and professor of French at New York University, RICHARD SIEBURTH is currently at work editing a book on Ezra Pound and French literature and culture for New Directions.

CHARLES SIMIC has published twelve books of poetry. In the spring of 1989 Harcourt Brace Jovanovich will bring out his prose poems in a collection entitled *The World Doesn't End.*

Recent books by GARY SNYDER include *Passage Through India* (Grey Fox, 1984) and *Axe Handles* (North Point, 1983). He has published six books with New Directions, including the 1975 Pulitzer Prize-winning poetry collection, *Turtle Island.*

A cultural critic of world renown, GEORGE STEINER is a regular contributor to *The New Yorker* and the *Times Literary Supplement* and is the author of such seminal works as *After Babel: Aspects of Language and Translation* (1975) and *On Difficulty &*

Other Essays (1978), both available from Oxford University Press.

Director of the Jack Kerouac School of Disembodied Poetics at the Naropa Institute, ANNE WALDMAN is the author of over twelve books of poetry, including *Makeup on Empty Space* (Coffee House, 1983), *Skin Meat Bones* (Coffee House, 1985), and *The Romance Thing* (Bamberger, 1987).

Forthcoming from Schocken in HARRIET ZINNES's translation is *Blood & Feathers: The Selected Poems of Jacques Prévert*. Also soon to appear is a collection of her short stories from Coffee House Press.